Damie

The Battle of Rainbows

Kevin Solomon Missal

DIAMOND BOOKS

SMS New Book at
9911044500 for Alert

ISBN : 978-81-288-3491-2

© Author

Publisher	:	**Diamond Pocket Books (P) Ltd.**
		X-30, Okhla Industrial Area, Phase-II
		New Delhi-110020
Phone	:	011-40712100, 41611861
Fax	:	011-41611866
E-mail	:	sales@dpb.in
Website	:	www.diamondbook.in
Edition	:	2011
Printed by	:	Adarsh Printers, Delhi- 110032

Damien Black The Battle of Lost Ages
By - *Kevin Solomon Missal*

Acknowledgement

Thank you God.

There are many people whom I want to thank as they had conjured their precious time to support and guide me. I would like to thank my dad, Leslie Missal who is the 50% holder of this book as he had faith in me and devoted his time. I also want to thank my mom, Jyotsna Missal,without her positive attitude, the novel would have been incomplete.

I am obligated to my friend Saday, who gave me ideas of the novel. Thanks to my brother, Ryan, who gave me his views of how a reader would enjoy a fantasy novel. Thanks to my friends: Ujjwal Bansal, Lakshay Yadav, Piyo Haroldu Jaiman, Alan P. Sam who always listened to my weird, crazy stories despite how stupid it was. I want to thank Tanya Malik for always being positive and excited about my stories. Roshan sir, for all the motivation and encouragement he gave.

In addition to this, I want to thank Ashok Dogra, Dhananjay Singh (Professor of South Asia University), Shivraj who guided me how to go about publication of the book. Special thanks to Shibani Missal for the contribution towards the book. To both my paternal and maternal grandmothers who continually supported me with their prayers and blessings.

– Kevin Solomon Missal

Preface

How the book came into being?

This book was just unexpected. I never thought that it would be published, plus I never even thought that this book would ever be written. The point is that lately during my summer holidays, I was intrigued in writing a non-fiction work which unfortunately wasn't that good plus was really small. So I thought just for the fun sake (as I didn't have much holidays left) I started writing the overview of a book: *Justin Storm the Slayer*. It made me feel really good. Battling monsters and standing as heroic was all in that overview. Later on I realized that Justin Storm's character has taken a turn into a darker skeptic, which made me come upon a name 'Damien Black'. The name Orpheus which was in the overview of *Justin Storm the Slayer* had now changed into Osiris, and the character Maggie changed into Athena. So when I started with the name Damien Black and the story which was already in my mind, I felt that this novel is going to be awesome. The feeling came because I was confident about this novel, and I had fun writing it. So my dad after listening to this Damien Black story said that it should be definitely published because it has a story line which can fascinate a reader. After getting positive reviews by most of the family members and also from the outsiders, we approached the publishers. This is how the book came into being.

How the idea came?

The idea came when my young friend Saday had foretold after finishing the Percy Jackson series: "There are no books left on heroic fantasy like Harry Potter or Percy Jackson." Then later on, my brother Ryan Mario Cardoza after watching some of fantasy movies said, "There is no novel or a movie which is stuffed with magic and enhanced fantasy." This gave me another idea — but not the entire plot was formed till then. Ryan also said, "There is no intelligent action in movies or novels these days." This made my mind work more.

As I know that Percy Jackson and Harry Potter series are unforgettable, I also know that many fantasy readers want more heroic fantasies. This made me form a plot of Damien Black which was darker, magical and romantic. Creating the world of Damien Black wasn't easy. The ideas were vivid but quite crazy and even stupid at some point. The narration done by Damien Black who is a teenager cannot be done better than a teenager himself. This made me write in first person style.

Then making the story more complex is to make the readers enjoy and at the same time scratch their heads, saying, "Hmmm…what the heck just happened?"

The idea of including fantasy creatures was to make the readers enjoy many adventures which the characters face. The idea of dream sequences came because I wanted to keep the reader guessing.

All the ideas that I have captured from here and there have made me form a complete *Damien Black* story.

Contents

What lays further, it's just a matter of fantasy.
— Kevin

Damien Black

Elena

Trojan

Athena

Lucifer

Azazel

Osiris

Nosferatu

Chapter - 1

The Lame Beginning

I ran.

It was something that I wasn't really good at...but when a group of Mermaids with ferocious teeth, mammoth fins and slimy naked bodies are attacking you—well, you don't have much choice.

Osiris and Athena were left inside the diminutive circular boat. Osiris was trying to stab the gamboling Mermaids by his staff's serrated side, and Athena was growling and masticating their skins off.

I was at the shore. My body was soaked with saline water, and my hair was all sticky with tar. My body felt numb, and my heart felt as if it was going to leap. I wasn't used to this Mermaid fights and battles. It really freaked me out.

My Beretta 92 was in my hand, and I aimed at one of the Mermaids who were assailing and endeavoring to break the boat. Honestly speaking, I wasn't good at shooting also. It was just my luck that whenever I shoot, the bullet hits the monster.

BAM!

The bullet was clobbered at the galloping Mermaid's fin.

The Mermaid's attention was now on me. They all looked at me with those rounds, silky beautiful eyes, and gave a daunting expression at me. Okay, now I'm darn sure that they are going to obliterate me!

They immediately swam towards the shore, leaving the boat alone now.

They refrained. They couldn't enter the land. Okay so now, I have an advantage. Mermaids can't enter land because they wouldn't be Mermaids then. I pointed my gun at one of the she fishes. For a brief second, I saw their innocent, loathsome faces and I found magnificence.

I wanted to throw down the gun and join them inside the water. And so I did. I left the gun on the sand, and walked towards them. They were all smiling at me with childish expressions, waving at me and calling me in sweet, melodious tone, "Come sire, come!"

I had entered the shallow water. I could feel my legs on the corals and the sea ground. But all I cared was their malevolent faces, showing glimmering beauty and their marvelous pulchritude. They took my hands...and then...

"NO!" Someone shouted from the sea.

I looked up and saw Osiris had yelled.

I came back to senses, and saw four Mermaids around me, smiling ferociously. I was hypnotized by their innocent, baby like faces, and now just due to that I am going to drown with them.

They caught my legs and pulled me down inside the depths of water. Fortunately, I had closed my breath, and I had time to come back on surface for air. The Mermaids were taking me down. Their fists were too strong to writher away. I kicked one Mermaid's head and she fell down at the bottom of water. Then I swam for the surface but then a

Mermaid approached. Her eyes were glaring at me deeply.

She kissed me tightly.

I was not ready for what happened. It was unexpected and unpredictable. So I kissed her back (not because I wanted to but because I could get some air from her mouth). Someone started pulling my legs and then I realized: They were planning this out. They had distracted my mind by kissing.

I was suddenly pulled down to the depths.

A string of light energy came towards the gathered Mermaids at the bottom. They all left my arms and legs, and rushed all around the sea, just to be away from the light. I don't know what that light really was, but it was coming towards me and I had to save myself. I swam at the surface…and finally grasped for breath.

"Oh my freaking gods," I muttered.

Osiris and Athena were now on the shore, calling me out. I swam forward, and approached the shore, with my body much heavier than before (maybe because of the saline). I just panted hard, catching for breath.

I sat down on the sand, and pulled my knees to the chest and grabbed it hard. It felt good now. It felt as if everything was in content.

Osiris and Athena sat beside me. Athena was sitting and putting her head down on the sand. Then Osiris spoke, "Did the light scare them off?"

So Osiris had assisted me in defeating the Mermaids by sending off a quick wisp wizard light who repels any she-fish. Not cool. It was because I didn't scare those sea monsters by myself. I asked, "Did you get what you needed?"

He showed me the small inch sized bottle which had red liquid, squeezed in it. He nabbed, "the magic potion with ingredients of a Mermaid's blood which can give us the long durability inside water. In another words, we will have gills to breathe in water for few extra minutes according to the drops we keep in usage."

I stood up on my feet, giving a look around the view, and by asking, "Osiris, I never asked you—where the hell are we?"

"The sea which you see in the front is Mediterranean and right now...we are at the coast of Libya."

That was my first mission.

Chapter - 2

Departing Sucks!

I wasn't a normal teenager. I was different.

My story began the day when I was departing from my former home with my uncle-cum-guardian—Osiris.

We were shifting our clothes, our weapons and our books inside the bags. Then we took out the bags, climbed down the aisle, walked past the courtyard and kept the bags inside the 1950's Jensen trunk. The car was already half broken.

I helped Osiris with his study room material. He had different sorts of potions, wands, books (which shouldn't be touched as it could eat you—literally) and also some ragged turbines, old pants, tattered cloaks, and battered hats.

Osiris had strictly ordered me that I should not touch any of his study room materials, or something wicked would happen. In another words, he really didn't like people touching his wizardry stuff.

So indirectly I'm indicating you that he's a wizard or sorcerer (he likes himself to be called sorcerer other than wizard). But not only that, he's a *professional* sorcerer having enhance knowledge about everything (omniscient, you can say), tricks which a normal warrior or a barbarian do not even know. He has also won many battles against different creatures and received Gold Medal for Sorcery and Magic.

I took the brown colored large box, and grabbed it tightly, flapping my arms around it. I went towards the car, opened the trunk, and kept the box inside.

The box contained all the sorcery stuff Osiris had...except the magic potion. I didn't know where the potion was. Maybe it had fallen by me mistakenly. I must find before Osiris finds out.

"What are you searching, Damien?" Osiris had immediately come in front of me, and scared a heck out of me.

"Whoa," I stepped back.

"What happened?" He asked, and looked down where my head was pointing. "Did you lose something?"

"Uh..." I stammered. "Y-your p-p-potions,"

I had known that Osiris' most precious possession was the potion which he collected and sometimes created. And losing it somewhere was what I really didn't fancy.

"Potions...the sorcery potions, aren't it?

I nodded my head.

"It's here, kiddo."

He pulled his black leather overcoat, revealing his dark red waistcoat, which had numerous bottle holders attached like a honeybee is attached to his hive. The holders were filled with bottles which were full of multi colored water or liquid and they were capped tightly with a rubber cork.

"Is it safe that you are keeping it here?" I asked indigently.

"Of course—as long as these little babies of mine are with me...they are entirely safe." He grinned, and then went towards the driver's side. "Anyways, say bye to your former home." He pointed at the long brown cottage with a chimney which no longer popped smoke out.

I wanted to wave my former home beamingly, but that would be just plain stupid. I would miss this house. It had unforgettable memories.

Osiris sat inside the blue tinted car, and yelled, "Let's go kiddo!"

I gave one last look at the cottage. I went back and sat inside the car where a womanly voice smirked at me saying, "Don't be emotional, Damien." And the voice wasn't of Osiris.

I looked back to see Athena. She was sitting uprightly with her head straight, brown smoky eyes wide, gold hairy body glinting.

She was my pet. She was a Golden Retriever. Well, but one thing was strange about her. She was also different like me. She could talk.

Osiris had said that she was an anthropomorphic female dog. He had told me about these anthropomorphic things. It means that a non living or an animal has human characteristics in them and Athena had human talking characteristic.

It was sometimes funny when I saw a serious talking dog. It always reminded me of the TV show, *Family Guy* who had a dog named Brian and who talked gulped vodka and scotch and even smoked cigarettes.

So once again, I started laughing when I saw Athena talking. Athena gave a grim look at me, and then a helpless look at Osiris saying:

"He has started it again!"

Osiris grinned at her saying, "Uh…don't worry…he's not used to it yet."

Then he glided the gear at the position, accelerated the car—and we headed towards our new home in—South County.

Chapter - 3

Twisted Dreams

I found myself inside a garden. I couldn't make out much of the landscape due to the intense light which hit my eyes.

I looked around, and saw the bright sun which glimmered with intense fury. I even saw the oak trees which stood near a boulder.

Everything was bright and beautiful. I felt as if I was in Heaven.

The grasses were soft and the leaves were quite dark. It was everything where a normal person would want to live.

But it was a dream…am I right?

I looked around, trying to stay away from the heavy brusque flashes of sunlight. I walked front, near the boulders which at end met a huge meadow covered with bushes and thorns and trees and woods.

I sat under the oak tree, next to the branches, whilst my jeans were brushed harshly on the grass. I folded my arms and kept my head under the shadows which were provided by the rustling leaves.

I didn't know where I was exactly. Am I dead and that

is why I'm in Heaven? Is it just a fragment of my vivid imagination? Is it *Paradise* where Hunters have an afterlife?

But I don't see my parents or my other fellow kindred anywhere. This place is isolated, empty—but filled with beauty.

I woke up in another dream!

I popped my eyes and saw myself standing on the marble flooring. I looked around, trying to figure out, where the heck am I? Then I saw it.

It was a hospital.

But this hospital wasn't a big, newly fashioned hospital. It was compact and small, with few doctors and nurses. It also had a reception where a fat woman was sitting and checking something on the computer.

I came towards her, and asked, "Excuse me…where am I?" She didn't reply.

She acted as if I didn't even exist in front of her. I waved at her, shouted in a hoarse pitch, and thumped my feet— but no improvement. She wasn't even paying attention towards me.

I have no idea of where I am and what I am doing here. Something is wrong, something is pretty darn wrong.

I look around for a brief time, trying to see if something I'm missing out, if something that can tell me that why I am here and where I am. Is this a dream like before? Is it the *out of body experience* which I'm having right now?

If it is *out of body experience* then how come it had happened with me? Am I dead?

I felt something in my stomach as if something had just grinded inside me. I looked down at my torso and saw a *hand*. The hand had been passed through my stomach and was giving few folders to the receptionist.

I looked back — seeing a doctor with huge black spectacles whose hand was inside through my torso. Then he pulled his hand back and walked towards the small corridor as if nothing had happened.

Now why this just happened?

I was scared. Am I dead? Am I a ghost right now?

I'm a Ghost!

A freaking ghost or a spirit!

I shouldn't freak out. Osiris had told me about this. This is just a dream. I am just entangled in my dream. And the only way to end this dream is —

I pinched myself on the arm.

I stood there, trying to see that if something had happened and that I had woken up from my dream. But, well, I was wrong. I was still inside the realms of my dream — and felt more stupid than before.

Just then, a doctor paced towards the reception. I moved alongside. The doctor was panting and sweating. He was tall and old with a little moustache above his upper lip.

He spoke in a very rapid way. "Anita Black, the wife of Timothy Black is admitted in ward 22. Please write this in the register and admit her immediately. Anita is going to bear a child. I'm taking care of it. But if you see Dr. Robbins, please inform him to come inside that ward. Okay?"

"Yes doctor."

"Good…and I need Nurse Wellington immediately with some of her more mates. We must not delay." He didn't even farewell, and sprinted towards the same corridor in which the first doctor did.

I stood there as if nothing had happened — whistling and biting my nails…

Timothy Black, Anita Black…hmmm!

Wait a minute!

They are my parents!

I immediately sprinted towards the corridor, and saw so many rooms. Every room was occupied with patients and nurses and one doctor. Some doors were closed whilst some weren't and I could see the treatment, which the patients were getting.

Finally, I arrived at Ward 22 which was the last ward in the corridor. The door was closed. I have to picklock the door, but how?

Hmmm…the door is locked.

I stamped my head. I am so freaking stupid. I'm a spirit right now, I can easily go through this door, and actually I can pass through any door or any obstacle.

I passed the door, and saw a doctor talking to the nurse in the side, next to a large monitor. On the bed, there was a woman with chestnut brown hair, and fair skin. Her eyes were almond and her mouth was red.

She was my mother. I couldn't believe it.

She was covered in a white sheet while she held a tall man's hand tightly.

The man was a shadowy character with dark brown eyes, thick bushy brown hair and a long cupid face. He was my father, I can make out from some pictures which Osiris had showed before.

"I can't believe—we are having a kid." Mom said, smiling softly at dad.

"Yes—it's a boy, am I right?"

"Hmmm…yes. The City Scan had showed it would be male." Mom replied. "Have you decided a name?"

"I have but aren't you deciding?" dad asked.

She paused, closed her eyes, and said. "I have left this decision to you."

"Then…uh…his name would be Damien. Damien Black."

I was intently listening to their normal conversation. It

felt so real. It didn't even feel like a dream. Maybe this is all been showed me for some reason.

Then it happened.

The entire view of my parents chatting with each other started to roll. Everything gobbled as if someone was eating the fragments of my dream. Then the entire scene of which I was seeing disappeared and I stood in darkness.

To my surprise, I was floating in mid air, and everything was dark and full of blackness. I couldn't see a thing. Maybe I was stuck in some port hole.

Then immediately I found my legs approaching the ground, and a new scene started producing in front of me as if someone is enabling my sub conscious memories in front.

The scene engulfed and I found myself in a new landscape. Maybe I was in some sort of house.

The house was small, dark and compact. It didn't have rooms or bathrooms. It was filled with dust and smoke. The chimney was broken, and the fire planks were scattered on the wooden floor. There were few weapons kept aside in the dark cavern which was next to the cupboard in front of the entrance door.

For a while, I could hear the chirping of a bird, and humming of sea breezes. Then, something grumbled and crumbled.

The crooked noises were coming from the entrance. It thumped, then bashed open.

I saw my dad, running away from the door as if something was repelling him.

A strange shadowy ghoul approached. The ghoul's face was covered with a dark hood, and he wore a long overgrown cape around his body. His hands and his face and his entire body weren't visible.

A shine of glint appeared from beneath the cloak, and I

noticed—they were the ghoul's teeth—point, smirked, and bloody.

"You shall be dead!" The ghoul said in a cold voice which gave me sudden wisps of chills. "You shall live not thou more!"

From beneath the cape's sleeve, he produced—oh my gods—his hand. His arm wasn't normal. It was bony, but wasn't totally bony. It was also covered with half pieces of mass and meat, and blood dropped from it. He pointed his bony, gruesome finger at my dad, and whispered, "May Underworld have pity on you!" A shine formed around his finger, like a fog, and then the fog sort of changed into a huge blue electric ball. The ghoul whispered omens and shot the ball at my dad's chest, collapsing him down on the ground, breathless and exhausted.

I shrieked in pain and misery…but…

The same thing happened.

The scene was gobbling as if someone was swallowing the entire picture at once, and leaving me in the darkness, floating again.

"Damien!" Osiris made me wake up.

I popped my eyes, and looked around. I saw Osiris and Athena staring at me, unbelievably as if something had happened.

Droplet of water came on my hand, and ran through down the arm. I touched my face, and the same water was all over. I was sweating.

I even felt something pounding inside my chest. It was my heart. I had a nightmare—a bad, bad, bad nightmare.

But how could I remember so many things?

I looked around, seeing that Osiris had halted the car near the main road, which met the forest. I even saw the forest which was covered with vines, hanging and dripping

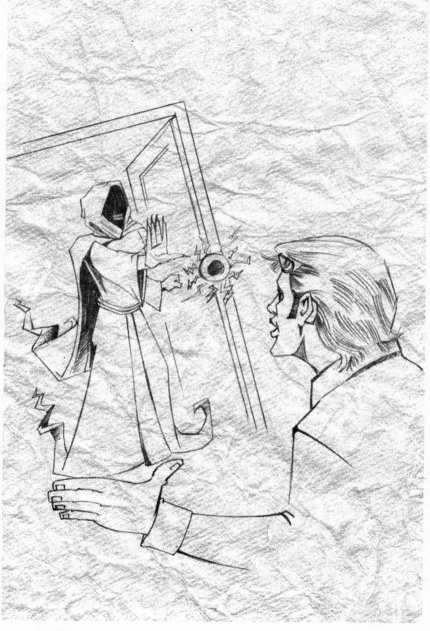

from the bushy canopies, and meeting the low branches, ending with the roots.

The grass on which the trees were embedded was dark and remorseless, having tiny droplets on them as if someone had drained potty mouth of water on it.

I could hear many different sounds which came from the forest. I couldn't make out the owner of voices but I assume that they are animals.

"Are you all right?" Athena asked, as she licked me on my cheek.

I rubbed my cheek disgustingly but then I remembered that Athena's saliva has a power to cure any injury, illness, or disease immediately if it is used in rightful proportions.

"What had happened, kiddo?" Osiris asked.

He immediately took my arms, and put his two fingers on my wrist—calculating my throbbing pulses, whilst I said:

"I had a bad dream."

He left my wrist and nodded his head to Athena. Then he said, "You were asleep for four hours, Damien. It felt as if you were in coma. We tried to wake you numerous times but you weren't getting up or anything—you just laid there with your eyes closed. We checked your heart, and we found that your heartbeat was at zero."

"What do you mean by zero?"

"You were *dead* for four hours, kiddo." Osiris answered, as he narrowed his eyes.

"How can this happen?"

Athena notched her nose, and spoke to herself, murmuring: "Possible Hypnosis that it could be near death experience or out of body experience. The both experiences are related. They both happen when a person skips many heart beats."

I asked, "b-but...uh...are you sure? How can it happen?"

"What kind of dream did you have?" Athena asked.

"I saw…" and I told them everything. I told them about my parents who were in the hospital before the bearing of me, then I saw my father dying by a ghoul, but I didn't tell them about the Paradise for some unknown (no idea) reason.

Osiris said to me, while turning his head to Athena, just thinking whether he is sure about his theory. "Maybe it was just a dream. Maybe it was a fragment of your imagination which entangled into many knots. Hunter does always encounter these sorts of problems."

Athena nodded her head. "Osiris is right. But what really astounds me is that, how come you know that your father was actually killed by a ghoul who was Death himself?"

"The personification thing—the Grim Reaper himself,"

"Well yes!" Athena replied. "Osiris…" she turned to my guardian and said. "Maybe this isn't just a dream. Maybe someone is trying to connect him to the past of his life by applying *Dream Travel*."

"You might be right. Dream Travel can happen if someone is performing himself as a medium between the dream and the person. Dream Travel has its conditions. It can psych your mind and blow it." Osiris said. "How was Death dressed?"

"How was Death dressed?" I repeated the question as if I was stupid and was trying to figure out the question properly. "He was in black cloak and dark hood or something…"

Athena immediately interrupted saying, "Did he have his scythe by which he takes away his victims?"

"No, not really…"

Osiris looked at Athena, and shook his head. "Then our assumption is wrong. Maybe it could be just a dream.

Maybe this dream or a nightmare had happened due to the collective yet shortage knowledge of your parenthood which created its own dimension and made most of us in belief." He chuckled, but it wasn't a happy chuckle like before. "This happens a lot with Hunters."

I could make out by Osiris façade expressions that he was trying to be positive about all this. But something was fishy, as Osiris put the car into gear (I saw his hand shivering vigorously) and accelerated, driving down the main road.

I looked at Athena, and narrowed my eyes. Her expression was...hmmm...expressionless, and her eyes were not even blinking. She was trying to hide all the fishy fear inside her so I could not make out but the way she looked blankly at the car window, I knew that something was ultimately wrong.

"By the way...why was my father killed by Death or so called Grimm Reaper, eh? I thought Death appeared when a person cheats death."

"Uh...hmmm...uh..." Osiris was plainly thinking and mesmerizing of how to give the statement. "Uh...well...Death was working with Azazel, the Demon of Darkness."

"I thought Death never works with anyone."

"We thought the same, kiddo." Osiris grunted. "But as you know, we found out that Death itself works with Azazel."

"That's something new," I muttered. "Anyways...these dream...do they happen a lot?" If they do, then obviously I will not sleep as those dreams looked really *real*."

Athena replied to that question, "Not always. When it is really important, then only it happens and we think that someone is *purposely* showing you these things."

"Is that so? Why is that?"

"For some purpose, some reason. But that's just

hypnosis; we are not sure, Damien. So we have to be silent about that till then. And anyways, Hunters have an ability to lose themselves inside their dreams which are half true and half not. There are many assumptions. Until the fact happens, we can't be sure of anything."

Okay, I didn't understand the entire thing what my talking dog just said. But yeah, I just understood that these dreams are just dreams which look real due to my freaky ability.

As Osiris drove towards the centre of huge forests and greenery, huge sheets of water poured down the windows. Athena popped her head out from one of the side windows, and opened her mouth, by which her tongue was floating in the air. She was acting like a typical dog which she actually wasn't.

When I look back, about the dream, I know that something is bitterly fishy. It is because they are the fragments of my imaginations.

Osiris never tells me about my parents, about my life, about myself. It is all mysterious. He has just explained that I am part of a Legion called the Hunters who keep the balance between good and evil.

. He somewhat told me that there is an Underworld which is parallel to our world (I know…quite like a fantasy book, right?) and which is controlled by Werewolves, Vampires, Goblins, Demons…and etc. All the creatures in mythology or in real are situated in Underworld.

We call them the Dark Creatures and they have the ability to come into our world through a portal and create chaos. The people like me (Hunters which I say) prevent this chaos.

But now (as Osiris says) that the incoming of beasts and monsters are now stopped because of some unknown reason (Osiris does not know which is quite surprising as he knows everything).

Osiris assumes that it is because of the new leader the Underworld had elected who calls himself the Demon of Darkness or in another words Azazel.

I have never seen him, and honestly speaking, I don't want to see him.

But Athena's theory is that Azazel isn't up to small damages on Earth (like sending monsters and creating destruction), he is up to something *really* big.

Osiris has also said that I am the last bloodline of Black's (of my family, if you say) which is the strongest and the most powerful family of Hunters. Our family had started the Hunter Legion (Yea, I was shocked).

That's cool, but that isn't really cool as I have to bear the tension of being a stupid guy who hunts supernatural creatures which come from another world.

He never told me about my parents. He always said that my parents wanted themselves to be confided from their child. Now what kind of parents would want this?

And so that is why, I (secretly) tried to find out about my parents which led me into some things. First of all, I learnt secretly that I was born in St. Cross Hospital in New York, and then I learnt that my father was killed by Death itself (I learnt it before Osiris had told me about it).

And maybe that is why I'm having so many wicked dreams. Whatever small information I'm trying to find about my parents, my subconscious is creating its own scenery and dropping me in that scenery.

As what Athena had said. Hunters create their own dimension with their half information of mind. This is really scary, really, really scary, I mean.

But why Osiris was shivering about this?

Osiris had always been mysterious about my parental

affairs or my destiny affairs. He always told me half information about everything. He had told me the reason. It was because, a mind cannot take burdens so many at one time, and everything should be told at the rightful timing.

Right now, he had told me that we are going to South County to find a kid who's also a Hunter like me. And why is that?

"Because there is shortage of Hunters on Earth now," I remember his statement.

So now, altogether, we will go, establish ourselves inside our new home, find the Hunter, and go to next destination which would be...I don't have a clue.

So that is what my life is, filled with magic and wonders, alongside come demons and dark arts. I could have said, "Hey...I'm Harry Potter." But being like Harry Potter really, really sucks.

"Have we reached South County?"

"It's right in front of you," Osiris smiled.

The anxiousness which was before on his facetious face was now long gone.

I looked at front...and just mumbled, "South County, here comes your new rail."

Chapter - 4

Was It Love?

South County wasn't what I expected it to be. Actually I really didn't expect anything from South County. I had seen it geographically and had noticed that it was at the East of Kansas which means that it would be like a small barn with pigs and buffaloes.

But well, I was wrong.

When our Jensen rode towards the main road, downwards, I saw the huge town (or a village) which wasn't mammoth but was suitable for us.

There were no skyscrapers (duh, it's a town) and there were small one storey buildings, attached to each other. There were few roads which rode along each other, being twisted altogether. The road ended at the woods which were huge and only the canopies were visible.

The bobbing street lights were tall and almost nine feet high, standing on the walking path.

"I feel as if I'm Isabella Swan and I'm approaching in Forks, Washington where I will fall in love with a Vampire." I chuckled, as well as Osiris did.

Athena looked blankly at us and said, "Your immature wit didn't humor me, Damien."

"Why are you always stiff and piff?"

"Is piff a word, Damien?" Athena scowled.

"Whoa, calm down...it is not...but who cares, right?" I grinned. "And by the way, enjoy life. You always stay grim and always cribber about every single thing."

"Our enjoyment starts when we are dead, Damien." Her womanly voice gave such a formal, mature touch. "When we are alive, we have norms and tasks to perform deliberately."

Athena was always a dog from the start. I mean, I thought that she would be some woman who was cursed by a witch and was transformed into a dog who talks. But my thoughts were really stupid.

As far as I know, Osiris had recalled that Athena was a normal dog when she was given powers by a witch. I haven't seen her powers till now (except the talking thing which isn't really a power for me).

We entered the slide road, where some small town cars were roaming. Some were parked near different shops and stations. The shops were really different, as because only some shops were renowned and others were just...homemade.

There were no McDonalds either!

We entered another road which on one side was filled with different varieties of shops, and while on other shop there was only green grass where some farmers mended the grass, and cows grazed.

"So which house are we going to live?" I said.

I saw many small apartments in some first storey buildings. There was a small resort with spa too. I saw small cottages at the little outside of town.

"The creepiest of all houses."

"As usual," I whispered to myself.

Athena said, "I'm hungry."

"Me too," I added.

Osiris didn't reply and then turned the car, and parked near the huge lamp. We got out and found ourselves standing just next to a huge subway station.

Athena grumbled, "I doubt that this would be having fresh subways."

I patted her head roughly and said, "Uh...don't be so negative, lad."

"I'm not a pirate, Damien." Athena gritted her teeth, as she walked in front of us towards the restaurant door.

Osiris opened the door, and we all three came in the restaurant, sat down, and looked around the empty vacant place.

The place was very mediocre. I don't mean like it was dirty and smelly. It had fresh smell of subways; it was even neat with a fragrance of naturalness.

But the entire place was vacant as if the restaurant was closed long before. The chairs were kept on the table, and the lights were dim as if the owner of this restaurant was trying not to lose electricity. The flooring was marbled with different colors, and the walls were colored in different colors.

I went towards the empty counter, and tried to find someone who could assist us in getting our stomachs filled with thick food. But in front of me, I could only see a cashier which was switched off, a bell, and a register. Behind the counter was the kitchen which was visible as the glass was transparent.

I rang the bell.

No sound.

I looked back and waved hopelessly at Osiris and Athena, mouthing "Let's go, the restaurant is opened from outside but closed from inside." But I don't think Osiris and Athena understood what I was mouthing as they mouthed, "Good, keep it up."

I narrowed my eyes on that misconception.

I turned my head to see the empty counter again...and...

WHOA!

My jaw fell down, my eyes popped wide, and my hair (just imagining) electrocuted. My heart was pounding out, and I was barely scared that it would fall down and break into pieces.

I saw a...

Girl!

She was standing behind the counter, with her glistening black hair tied in a small ponytail, black darkish eyes making me fall inside a porthole of beauty and magnificence, and curved soft lips that gave a slight smile, when she said: "Welcome to Sanchez Subway Station also known as SSS. Here we sell Mexican, American, Spanish subways."

"Uh...ah...hmmm..." And I said one of the most remarkable, intelligent things. "Lord of the Rings."

She narrowed her eyes in suspicious. "Beg your pardon?"

"Uh...no...nothing," I stammered. "Uh...ah...ah... please give me Spanish subway with an Italian, and capsicums should be cut in regular thin pieces giving a slight touch of elegance..." I ordered the entire menu for me, Osiris and Athena.

Chapter- 5

The haunted Mansion

"What was the cause of the stammering occurrence, Damien?" Athena asked. "Is it a dilemma of yourself which imbues you?"

"I really didn't understand what you said...but..." I replied. "I was scared. I looked at that counter girl, I felt scared. I don't know why."

Osiris gave a low chuckle. "Kiddo has a crush, eh?"

Athena licked her nose, and stood silent. I asked Osiris, "By the way, have the furniture's being settled and all, as we haven't shifted the previous furniture of our former home."

"The Gnomes headed by our favorite Bogart, Mr. Todd is assisting us in furniture stuff and settling stuff."

"You always take help from them, eh?"

"They are the best, uh." Osiris smiled.

For a while, I didn't notice that I had left South County, but when I saw the marvelous greenery, and the huge landscape which met the dawning sun at the horizon.

I looked at front and saw a huge house, maybe it was a

mansion, but was incredibly old and creepy. So Osiris was right. We were going to live in a huge, isolated, creepy house. Whoa.

But that didn't really astound me the most. As we came nearer the house, which was few paces away from the town (which means that many of the townsfolk couldn't see our house much, and they could also not see the magical stuff we do), overlooking a small, withering river which galloped inside the woods.

Our house was more like a Haunted Mansion, but I really didn't want to say it in front of Osiris as we were ourselves haunted in front of normal humans.

The house ended in the huge bushy woods, and on the right side was a valley as I said, and on the left side was a small vacant farmhouse with a lock attached to it. But our Haunted Mansion had double hung window, wooden walls being gallfly constructed and by any means it would break if something would jab to it. The railings which were at the exterior, and near the entrance door, were made of pine, and were the best thing in the house. The tongue-and-groove decked porch roof and roof beautifully, but the cobwebs being jagged multipliable ruined the entire pulchritudinous of the top external.

Osiris halted the car, and stood next to the huge house. He looked down and touched the pastures which joined the front porch, and then simpered in amusement.

"What was that for?"

Athena vehemently enunciated, "He was inner vitiating the Protective Charm which Mr. Todd had sprinkled around the house, Damien."

"Oh,"

Well the Protective Charm was always useful and I had many times seen Osiris dredging the powder which wasn't visible by human eyes.

The wooden, creek door bashed open, and I found a huge Bogart coming with his marching servants of Gnomes.

Mr. Todd (whom I've seen frequently in many years) was in a black overgrown cloak, which touched the brisk wooden floor. His hood wasn't caped on his slimy, small head with pointy ears, white fluffy hair, dark brown brusque eyes, pure green disgusting skin and large ominous dishabille teeth.

All his servant gnomes were smaller than him, more scintillating than him, and more finicky than him.

They were all in small green uniforms; with a green small coat (I wonder where they get this extra, extra, extra, extra small size of dresses in shops), red bow tie, white gleaming shirt, brown soiled pant, and disheveled boots.

Mr. Todd grimed, "Oh hello, my little boogie Osiris, eh?"

"Hi," Osiris gave a low, unenthusiastic smile. "Is everything done?"

"Oh, yes!" Mr. Todd jumped in mid air, but fell down, as his leg got entangled in his long cloak, breaking his jaw. "OW, OW, OW!"

Athena was sitting upright on the planks, looking fervently at the humorous small Bogart.

One gnome helped him up on his feet, and then he covered his disfigured face with his hood, and sighed, saying "Well, well, well...what is the proffer Osiris?"

Osiris beamed, saying "Here...take this." He took out a potion bottle from his waistcoat, and kneeled down, handing it to Mr. Todd with apprehension. "This potion can make you invulnerable for a day."

"Wow," Mr. Todd's eye glistened with delight. "You are such a nice customer," He nabbed. "Any help in future, just summon me, eh." He then turned to his fellow gnomes, and yelled at them with ferocity. "Let's go you young

toddlers; we have to go to Mr. Baggy now." He divulged some words to himself.

The next second I know—he evanesced in mid air.

My eyes were humongous and inclusive due to consternation.

But then the astonishment went off, and we entered our new home...

Chapter - 6

First Day of School...
Can't Be Worse!

I woke up in the morning and found myself baffled about everything. Well, this confusion happens with me a lot for some reason, whenever I wake up. My head feels dizzy and uneven, and my body weak and feeble.

I snooze numerously (uncountable) and stretch my arms and legs tumultuously, until I get good feeling in my body.

The alarm was energetically ringing, as I shut it off, and then turned my face, and jammed it on the soft pillow, with one hand and one leg half falling down from my bed and down at the wooden slats.

Woof...woof!

My eyes bobbed open.

I leered, and found that Athena was the one who had disturbed my delightful slumber. She was smiling, when she said, "I postulate that you would be in deep lucid dreaming, which is satisfying you and professing you from the materializing life which you are in reality."

"What did you just say?"

She smiled, and then hunched her back, grabbed my pajama suit with her ferocious teeth, and pulled me with so might force, that I fell down from the bed and down at the red, silken, handloom carpet.

I was persisted to dress up for my first day for South County Academy. I brushed my teeth up and down, then sheepishly bathed myself, ruffled my hair by which it looked indecent, and then dressed myself.

I stood next to the mirror, and glared at myself. My eyes black as my father, were glistening with sleep, my body tall and tough with little muscles protruding from my shirt. I wore the single breasted waistcoat on myself which had a full vertical opening in the front.

I fastened my bag on my back, and so I went.

The entire day in school was okay-okay. No one knew me and no one paid attention to me. I went to the high school coordinator who gave me the time table slip and had told me to meet Elena, some prefect girl who can show me around the Academy and give me brief information about it.

The school from the exterior was big; actually it was the biggest building in the town having two storeys, plus a red shiny bricks which allured the entire landscape around it. In front of the school, there was a huge play ground for footballers, whilst just alongside stood a basketball court where some kids were playing.

There was a huge flag which hoisted and flapped due to the heavy adroit wind.

I walked past the corridor, and tried to find my locker, and then I had to find Elena. But before seeking the locker, I got confronted by a funny looking guy who had just leaped in front of me with a beaming, acoustic smile.

"HEYYYYY…you are the new kid, aye?" He brought his hand forward. "My name is Trojan, dude. Everyone or particularly family call me Duke. But anyways call me Trojan; I feel more Greek, mate." He winked.

I shook hands with him and tried not to act weird or something. So I was calm and decent, by which I asked him, "Can you tell me my locker?"

He took the slip, and guided me towards my locker. He opened it for me, and I thanked him for his assistance.

"Anytime, mate. By the way, you need any help—just you know, inform me."

"Sure."

I got a clear view of his face. First of all, I got a look at his goatee which covered his lower margin of the chin, and then I saw his green emerald eyes. He was too fair (unlike me as I was dusky) and much looked like British (also according to his fake American accent).

He was in loose clothes like a loose sweatshirt and loose badgered pants. He wore a large cap which covered his half head and he thought that he was looking cool and smart.

"Can you help me find…" I had forgotten that girl's name, and for that I had bestrewed my thoughts on the slip. "Elena, Elena Sanchez."

Trojan's cool behavior suddenly became stiff and stubborn, as he said, "You can't have her. She is someone else's."

"What do you mean?"

"I know that you like her. But I will not help in finding her and risking my life for that, huh." He chuckled in amazement.

I licked my lips, and said, "I don't like her. Heck, I haven't even seen her till now. I just want to know because the coordinator had said that she could assist me in some matters as she is a senior prefect."

Trojan did not believe about what I said, but still without speaking, he waved me to follow him. I did, and he took me up to the top stairs, where a clique was standing and chattering and battering with enthusiasm.

. "What is this?"

"This group is known as the Labyrinth."

"Why is that??"

"Because we get lost whenever we see them," Trojan smirked. "Anyhow…" he went towards the clique, and from the between, he called a girl out of the group…whom I had seen before.

She was familiar.

I was figuring out her face and I realized…*oh that subway girl!*

The girl who I stammered in front of—and now I was scared, because I had no clue that I would be able to batter out words when she will discuss something or converse something with me.

Trojan waved at me and then flickered to go out of the corridor where Elena and I stood in front of a huge clique which giggled and jiggled shyly.

She was in shorts and a small top. I think she does not like clothes as she barely wore anything on herself.

Her hands were occupied with books, but still, she said, "Hey, are you the stammering guy who met me yesterday?"

"Hmmm…yeah."

"So…you are the new guy, eh?"

"Why everyone is calling me the 'new guy'?" I emphasized.

"You will find out soon. But, as you have come, and you need my help—so why not tell something about this school." She smiled softly which gave eternal light to my heart, and I knew that my heart just skipped.

I exulted, "So you are going to tell me about architecture and the history of this boring building, eh?"

She shook her head negatively, and snatched my slip. She saw the slip, and said "Walk with me." I did as she said.

We walked, as she began saying "the architecture is boring so you have to skip that. The history is that Albert Einstein was the founder of this school, just kidding..." she sniggered. "Yeah, but some renowned personality in nineteenth century had found this. I really don't know who it was and so on, blah, blah, blah."

We passed the water tanker, and in front I saw two corridors being separated on either side by a huge glass window.

"But what really concerns you is..." she pursued her lips. "Dan!"

I was befuddled of what she said. "Dan?" I repeated. "And who is this Dan?"

"Dan stands for Daniel Mosby, son of this town's sheriff. He would make your life hell here."

"And why is that?" I paused. "Does he have some grudges against me?"

She gave a wistful looked, "He has grudges with every freshman. And honestly speaking, if he finds out that I'm talking to a *freshman*, he will of course kill you and throw your blood soak body inside the damp river which is near that haunted mansion."

Well, she was talking about my house—at least she knows about the existence of that house.

"I'm just kidding around. But..." she stopped her motioned body, and pressed one finger at my chest, saying

"You have to go according to Danny Boy's Rule Book. And as you seem very decent and not a nerd, I would help you."

"That's very kind of you, but what are the rules?"

She spoke in a hoarse pitch, "If you ever break rules, your head would be found in a dumpster. The first rule is, you can't talk too much with his girlfriend and I'm his girlfriend."

My heart leapt as if someone had kicked it hard. I don't know why I felt like this, but I was sure that my face had frowned in anger. "That means I had broken the first rule itself." I tried to remove the frustration and become witty.

She giggled slightly and then told me the further points. She told me that I should meet with Dan on first day, and introduce myself to him. Then she said about fighting with some random guy so I can show how capable I am in fighting (if I lose, I'm a nerd, if I win, I'm a jock). She also told if I become a nerd, he will trouble me a lot but if I am a jock, then I would become Dan's best friend.

"Now, as I've told you everything. So basically this is your Chemistry class in first period." She pointed at the room to which we stood parallel. "If you need any help about anything, just tell me. But you must clear out the issues with Dan first."

I just nodded my head and smiled.

She winked, and then she went back to her clique.

For a while, I stood there, frozen, lips quivering, body trembling and I just realized:

Did I just have a conversation with that girl?

Chapter - 7

The Big High School Fight

"So you are ready, mate?" Trojan asked as we skated our feet towards the cafeteria.

The cafeteria was bigger than other classrooms. There were kids sitting and chattering and battering some stuff which wasn't audible as there were so many voices at once.

So before I caught up Trojan and told about the things which Elena had said. Trojan was excited about this all. He had said that he had won the jock and nerd game when he was a freshman in this school. But his importance is no more.

"I'm so freaking out, mate." We came to the cafeteria counter where a huge brusque lady stood, with her head slightly upright from the counter's transparent window.

There was a small section where foods were displayed. While we were getting food, he said, "See, first of all, when we will come to Dan. I will do the talking. You have to be silent all the time, you understand?" his voice was persuasive.

"Sure."

"Good, now let's go!"

We took our cafeteria tables, and indefinably walked

towards a group of soccer players (as I could see their soccer sweatshirts), who were quite disquietude in words.

Every soccer player was tough and muscular and faces like monsters that are going to erupt any second or so.

Trojan waved at them, "Hey!"

They all pirouette their faces, and gave repugnant expressions to...ME!

A curly haired, broad shouldered, lurid face guy stood who was the tallest of the group. He stretched his brows and said, "Hmmm...the freshman which I've heard about, eh?" He gave a spiff of attitude towards me.

"Oh yes, Dan." Trojan smiled feebly. "He has arrived for the test, you know — about the jocks and nerd."

"Well, I consider him a nerd right now only." Dan beamed at his friends who laughed hoarsely. "But anyhow, the rules are the rules." He came forward, and stood next to me, just few paces away from my head. "So you are tough, new bee?"

"Uh..." I wasn't scared; I just tried to be more coward right now as it is the best for me. "I have no clue," I gave a nervous chuckle.

"Hmmm," he pursued his lips tightly and gritted his teeth, saying. "Let's see then. You know what to do, right?"

"I have to beat up a random guy." I said.

He nodded his head in affirmation and said, "Hmmm...as you have given a lot of QUALITY time to my girlfriend," he eyes me angrily, and I knew possibly that I was dead. "Why not fight with Big Bob?"

Everyone in the cafeteria started vociferating in apprehension and aggression. I wasn't noticing before that all the kids were looking at me, and I also didn't notice before that Elena was watching me in anguish.

My heart was thumping (not because of the name BIG BOB but because everyone was looking at me, cheering and thinking that what would be my destiny in this school. Will I be a jock or a nerd?) And giving low shrieks.

Maybe the name is ironical. Maybe the Big Bob isn't really big and he's just some small nursery guy who is notorious for his volcanic name.

Well, my hypnosis was wrong.

It is because, in front of me, stood the most behemoth guy ever (in humans of course as I've seen a mammoth dragon, a walloping Basilisk and also extra large Gorgon with a fat tummy—but anyways...) who looked at me blankly.

His stomach was the most abnormal thing. He had eight slabs of mass, distending out like as if eight people are living inside it (No wonder!) and trying to get out.

"You have to fight him, new bee."

"Ah...sure."

I really didn't see Big Bob's face as his entire body was covered with the dropping, dismantling stomach.

I kept the food tray down, and stood next to him. I gave little crocks to my body, making it flexible.

Osiris had told me. Hunters are more powerful than humans (in physical, mental and spiritual way), so I had some hopes on myself.

But standing next to me, wasn't a human for me. He was a blob, a big blob. My thin body couldn't be compared with his...

BAM!

I was thrown back at the cafeteria table. A string of pain reached my spinal cord, and it started twigging badly. I got up, frowning, and massaging the spinal area.

Everyone hooted!

Big Bog walked towards me, with his dirty, sticky face being licked by his large enormous tongue.

I came towards him. I must think smartly. I can't just

punch him and kill him (as everyone would get fishy about me), so I must injure him in some other way.

I came from the back of his body. He took time to move his entire legs and his stomach till that I swung my foot at his legs, making him collapse on the ground—and it was done...one shot!

He was trying to move his body up but it was difficult for him. He stretched his arms and legs up, trying very hard, but no use. The weight of the body had hit the floor, and it would deductively take five men to make him stance once again.

Well, no one was volunteering for that.

I took his one stretched arm, and pulled him up (Yeah, I'm that powerful), making everyone astound around me in bewilderment.

Dan's mouth was like a big O and Elena's facial expressions showed too shock.

Big Bob said, "thank you for pulling me up," he hugged me hard, tightly and honestly speaking (not to be rude) I could feel his loose breasts and his huge abdomen.

Chapter - 8

An Abnormal Night

Dan befriended me with a grin on his face and embraced me tightly, welcoming me to come in his group (and even in soccer group but I wasn't interested, as I thought they would think that I'm too fast than a normal human).

I was allowed Danegal (Dan + Legal) to talk to Elena now. Trojan was surprised and for few following days he just stared at me, unbelievably.

But the most important thing was Elena. I don't know why, but I felt happy whenever I was around her.

In the next few days (I hadn't told Osiris about the strength I used on Big Bob as he always says 'Do not use powers on a human') I was getting much importance than before.

No one now cared to mess with me, and everyone gave a slight smile whenever I passed around them. I spent quality time with Elena also, trying to show that I was puzzled about every matter (which I wasn't) and asked her everything which made her close to me more.

Fortunately, I didn't have vivid, crazy dreams now, in which I went to past—maybe because I wasn't thinking about my family's past or maybe because I was less stupid than before.

That was one day…when something I found out.

"Something is wrong." Trojan uttered.

"What do you mean?" I catechized.

"Something is wrong with you, mate."

"What have I done?"

"You are different," he came closer, when I closed my locker, and clutched my books on to my chest. "You have something peculiar."

I was wondering that he felt that I wasn't human, and was like Spiderman (except that I could not stick to a wall and I can't swung pleasurably). But his eyes told that he was trying to figure out, but exactly couldn't.

"I don't know why—b-but something is wrong. I feel it." Trojan narrowed his eyes and studied my sweaty face which now became anxious. "I feel as if you are *like* me."

"Like you?"

I gave a glance to his loose, un-cool, indecent and disheveled personality, and I was darn sure, that I wasn't like him—at all.

"No, that's a wrong assumption, dude." I paused. "By the way, have you got any partner for High School Dance?" I wisped my brows up.

"Yeah, Stella," he claimed the name. "She's right there and I'm waving at her." Trojan winked at the red, curly haired girl.

I thought for a second. I can trust this guy. He's stupid (more than me), can be loyal to me plus he can help me also. "See dude…" I pushed along the group of lockers. "I have a crush on Elena," I whispered.

His eyes turned ellipsoidal in abnegation, but he kept his mouth shut.

I continued my talk, "But as I can't get her because she

has a dimwitted, idiotic boyfriend, I want you to fix me with a date."

I left his collar, and stood little pace away from him. He was bearing the shock which I immediately created in front of him, and he stayed frozen for two minutes exactly.

Then he spoke up:

"There is Jane, Trisha, Dahlia…they all like you."

"They like me?" I was shocked. "Whoa…"

"Because of me," he showed off. "Anyways, which one would you like?"

"Anyone of the three just is sure that it shouldn't be some ugly, retaliating girl."

"As you wish, captain," he saluted me and was going to depart when I got a hold of his shirt, and pulled him saying:

"What's with his pirate tone, eh?"

He didn't answer me. He just said. "Ahoy!" And left!

Back at the Haunted Mansion (yea, I literally started calling my creepy house Haunted Mansion), I found Osiris sitting in the patio which was a courtyard wrapped by an open sided terrace, at the apex, and it was covered with a pergola.

There were some plants which moved deliberately in every position, gripping each other, battling each other, and also kissing each other. They were plants which had been given a magical potion from Osiris Potion Collection. Now these plants were producing themselves very fast and giving some liquid which only Osiris can have.

Osiris was with his high technological Wiz computer which enables him to break the firewalls and hack into any computer easily.

Athena was sitting just next to him, looking out at the

bright sun which glimmered at her, and made her shinier than before.

"Hey, what are you doing?"

"We are trying to find the Hunter which is lost here." He was too studded in the computer and typing very fast, without even seeing the keypad and keeping his eye on the monitor.

"You haven't found him till now?" I was surprised, as Osiris was working a lot now days in researching. "Should I help you?"

"What do you desiderate, Damien?" Athena asked in a husky, female voice.

Osiris turned his head for the reply, leaving his search work away.

"Well, today is the school dance—so can I go?" asked I.

Athena laughed.

Osiris gave a slight smile. "I thought that you don't have to be attached to this school or to people in this school, kiddo. We came in this town to find the surviving Hunter. And you want to dance, eh?"

"He wants to jiggle-wiggle, Osiris." Athena beamed, and fell on her back, moving her hands and legs childishly.

"Come on, I haven't had fun since—since very long."

"Fighting demons and monsters isn't fun for you. Many kids are desperate to be like you."

"Fighting Dark Creatures is like a responsibility, Osiris. I feel suffocated as if I have made a commitment with someone to stay like this."

"Indirectly you have made." Osiris said, and he regretted what he said.

Athena immediately stood up, as well as my arm hair. "What do you mean 'indirectly you have made'?"

"Uh..." he looked with long, elongated eyes to Athena, so she could cover up the slipping words from Osiris lips but she stayed still, nervous. "Uh…I can't hide from you. So the honest answer is that your parents wanted you to be a Hunter as well. They had a choice, they could have let you go and make you live like a human, but they wanted you to follow their legacy."

"That's stupid!" I spouted beamishly.

He took my arm, and rolled my sleeves up to the elbow, and showed a Pentagon tattoo on my arm between the wrist and the elbow. The Pentagon had a cobra which had swindled itself inside the star.

"This isn't a stylish tattoo you have acquired from some Goblin tattoo guy. This is a mark which every Hunter has on his arm. And your parents were the ones who had created this on your hand to signify that you are a true blood Hunter and that you have committed your life as a Hunter in spite of your mother argued that you should be given a choice but your father was persistent."

"Why?"

"He had its issues!" Osiris replied in a non-confident tone.

"How can they take such a big step without even telling me?"

"They are your parents, kiddo. They know best of you."

"Why haven't you told me?"

"Because I didn't feel like telling before—everything has its own time, Damien. I can't just rush into everything I know."

Blah, blah, blah…

So I wasn't cool. I thought that having a tattoo of a cobra inside a Pentagon would be cool but I was wrong. It was a mark, created by my own freaking parents. I hate them.

"So what about the school dance? After a bad news, one gift is necessary."

"You are a clever smut, Damien." Athena spoke highly. "Taking advantage of the weak prospective which Osiris had just foretold, I am heavily impressed."

I smiled weakly. I was still really resented from my parent's choice. At least they should have consulted me and asked my opinion.

"Duel with me, kiddo, if you win, I'll let you go. If you'll lose, you have to help Peter then." He pointed at a green, disfigured creature with hairy head, dark black eyes, small, crooked body and huge boulder hands.

In another words he was a Goblin.

He was a house Goblin who was captured by Osiris himself, and he helps in making food, cleaning dishes, and emasculating the house.

"Sure!"

We came to the courtyard which was an enclosed area, opened up onto the sky, willowed by clouds.

The plants and the vines surrounded the entire court, but there was a small opening, a path, by which I and Osiris entered the large opening made of marbles.

Athena was on my side, and Peter was on Osiris side.

Peter was massaging Osiris neck, and was whispering some details. I kneeled down, and asked Athena, "Can you hear what Peter is saying by your dog ears?"

"Don't humiliate me by calling a dog. Anyhow, Peter isn't saying anything. He's doing it purposely to puzzle you." Athena spoke.

"Oh!"

"His deficiency trait is his way of defending every attack. Your strategy is that you must comprehend his attacks and puzzle him of which side you will hit him, in that way, he will not know your intrusion, and will try to be offensive. At that position, you must take the advantage and assault him on the armor."

"Whoa, you are good." I said.

I wore my armor which was made of real compact brass. I was given a sword made of Phoenix fire in Goblin's cavern.

He also wore the same, and clutched his special sword. My amenity was that Osiris was not as better in sword fighting and I was better as he had trained me in that way.

He was a good trainer, but I became better than him.

He came towards me with a spontaneous smile, stretching around the corners of his mouth which was covered with a French beard.

He jabbed the sword towards me, but I deflected it, and bucked it hard on his armor. He collapsed back, and stood up again in aggression.

He walked towards me. I tried to be offensive by stabbing my sword towards his armor but all he did was sneering it perfectly and without any trouble.

Then something happened. My brain started to work really rapid. My mind mesmerized every possibility and gave the details in front of my eyes.

I will hit his jaw with the hilt of my sword causing him deliberate damage, and then as he massages his chin, I'll kick him on the diaphragm making him snooze on the floor. This theoretical stealth postulate can occur due to exact right timing of my hands and legs.

Osiris tried to punch his sword towards my armor, but I rolled my body, he turned his face towards me, I punched his jaw, he moved back as if he didn't expect this attack. Then I immediately immersed a kick on his stomach which made him lose consciousness.

I came back to senses!

My head was paining brutally. I couldn't understand why. I saw Osiris on the floor, groaning in pain. Peter saw me with amazement as well as Athena also.

I just didn't know how it happened.

It was as if my consciousness was working rapidly than a normal person, and I had time to think and act stealth actions on another person.

Hey...but anyways, I was going to the party.

It was just a small nap which gave me the most horrific dream.

I was back at the beautiful landscape which I had mentioned about before. The gleaming sunshine poured its beauty on my skin and the frisky flowers which were being unstable due to the soft cool wind.

I was back at my dream *Paradise* but this time—I wasn't alone.

Where the boulders and the oak trees met, a gap which was dark, there a man stood, his face hidden due to the extensive shadow which made him invisible!

I came forward to have a good look at him.

He also came forward, and showed himself to me.

First of all, I was darn sure that it was an angel as he had huge galloping wings which were almost seven feet long and three feet wide but the color was dark black.

His eyes were red, and his pupils were white in between. He was in an Armani suit maybe, with a double breasted coat, single handed pants, rough, clean boots which gave a long elongated shape. His face was perfect, calm and not puzzled and nervous at all. His hair was combed properly and was oiled to the right margin.

The angel walked towards me with an expressionless face. I really didn't know how to react, so I stayed still, as I knew that this was my dream and that angel couldn't do anything.

And otherwise, he was an angel. He would not harm me, duh.

He sat on the rock which was nearest to me, and said in a low, husky tone. "Hello, Damien."

Did he just say my name?

Oh yes, he did!

"Who are you?"

"Right now, it does not matter of who I am and what I am." He blinked his eyes just once, and continued. "You can say that I'm a fabric of your imagination. You can say that I am a helper. You can say that I am a future teller. You can say me an angel. You can say me a man. I am millions of things, Damien. I am something which only comes to assist people in their dreams."

"So what are you doing in my dream?"

"I am giving you an evil omen, Damien Black. I know…" he paused, and low his head. "That you don't know me. But you must trust me. There's going to be an attack at the town's Hunter where your guardian is trying to find."

"And who is he?"

"He is someone who you have to find yourself. He isn't what you expect. He isn't who will just come in front of you and tell that he's a Hunter."

I narrowed my eyes in confusion. "You are not helping me at all. So the name 'helper' is cut off from the list. And second of all, I can't understand that why aren't you telling me that Hunters name and where is his location if you call yourself, so-called 'helper'."

He stayed calm and silent for a while, thinking deep and remorselessly. "Because time is something which you can't mess with, Damien — time is telling me that you will know the name itself. Be patient, you are impervious to patience, Damien Black."

That's really helpful. Now he's criticizing me.

"The dead are rising from the graves, Damien, to kill you and your partner. You must protect him in the school dance or you shall regret." He stood up, his face gleamed brightly.

He moved back towards the small gap between the boulders, when he turned, flapped his wings and said, "Osiris has many secrets which can change your life, Damien." He whispered. "You should be ready for the impeccable end."

He vanished.

I woke up!

I wasn't sweating now. I was feeling as if a breeze is whipping my chest and my shoulders. I gave a look around my scattered room, and found the window open.

Then I gave a look at my clock and found it was seven O'clock already. Oh, my gods! The dance would be starting in thirty minutes.

I raced up and down in the house, changing my dress, and wearing a long waist-coat, with a loose tie, pointed boots.

I started remembering what the angel in my dream had said. But the main question was—was I controlling the dream?

I wasn't sure. It was because, that time, in my dream self, I was thinking about Elena, but she wasn't there, instead a calm angel was. He was controlling my dream and I don't know why.

He was exhorting me with a bad news. I was going to find the Hunter today at the party. But who it would be? Stanley, Trojan, Dan…or Elena…

My hair rose up from my neck when a thought of Elena being a Hunter came in my mind. I was rummaging through the drawer to find my Dagger-Gun Holster which was gifted to me by Osiris on my fourteenth birthday.

I finally found it, and gave a low glow beam, when a voice said, "Why are you so frightened, Damien?"

It was Athena.

I stood up while scratching my neck in anticipation, and thinking what kind of excuse should I give to her. "I-I was thinking about…you know…the dance. Trojan has got a date for me, you know." I weakly grinned.

She narrowed her eyes, and spoke, "You know I can smell fear loathing in your body. Plus you are sweating which makes my case simple. You are lying. And why are you doing that?"

"Okay," I surrendered.

There was no use of lying to Athena. I know she will feel that I'm becoming a bit freaky, by which I'm having some unusual dreams, but still she was the one who had always taken care of me. She was like my mother— figuratively.

"Uh…I saw a dream…in which I saw that I will find the Hunter which Osiris is trying, seeking for so many days."

She raised her brows. "Very well…"

Very well…just very well?

"You are thinking that this is some stupid dream of mine that I'm having. But you know what? I'm having a feeling as if something really would happen."

She just nodded her teeth, "And why are you taking the guns and the dagger where you have to spend some intimate moments with a girl?"

She caught me again.

The dead are rising from the graves, Damien. You should protect you and your partner or you will regret.

I remember what that angel or that guy with wings said. It really horrified me. I wasn't ready for some protection, honestly speaking.

"Okay listen, I also had a dream that monsters will attack that Hunter. I have to protect him."

"So generous of you," Athena smirked. "Osiris!" She yelled at the back.

For a while, no one came. Then Osiris approached, with his hair ruddy and dirty.

"Give him the watch," Athena said.

"Why now?" Osiris cried.

"It is because, this is the right time." Athena eyed Osiris.

Osiris stood for a moment, then nodded, looked at me, and went back. He came a little while later, with a digital watch in his hand and handed me.

"This is a Wiz Watch, kiddo. If any danger lurks around you, just press that little red button and through the speaker phone we can converse and I will come with Athena for your help. The watch can also tell that where the monsters are. It will start beeping loudly when some danger is around, you understand?"

I nodded, and wristed the watch on my hand. I wore my holster, which was perfectly camouflaged inside my waist-coat.

"Are you ready if some monster approaches and tries to kill you?"

"Sort off," I wasn't ready.

My Beretta 92 Infinite Ammo pistol was on the right side, and my dagger which was made of a Minotaur's horn and which is convertible in a long thirteen meters sword, was on the left side.

"Am I looking handsome?" I asked.

Osiris gave me a huge smile, and Athena just nodded. She wasn't really good at smiling, otherwise.

As I was going—I heard Athena speaking...

"It has started!"

I was at the school dance which held in the basketball court. There were spotlights flickering on the court, and the DJ was playing weird, freaky songs.

Many students were dancing already and I was perfectly sure that I had arrived late. I descended some steps, and searched Trojan for a while.

I saw Elena dancing with Dan, and his friends, Ryan and Eric were dancing with their respective girls.

I was alone—felt kind of awkward.

I came off the dancing court, and looked around to see if Trojan is here or somewhere.

But honestly speaking, I was searching the missing Hunter. There were almost all kids on the dance court, and anyone could be a Hunter. I have to see carefully, with my eyes big as ever.

All I could see was Elena with her shoulder less red shiny dress, which looked way awesome. Her lips were shinier than the spotlights and her eyes gave the glimmering momentum.

Dan was an idiot. Dan isn't worthy for Elena.

Concentrate…Damn you!

So, Elena could not be a Hunter. She has such delicate and soft skin, how can she be some rugged, rigged Hunter who fights creatures from Underworld?

A thump on my shoulder came. I immediately looked back as if some creature had arrived—but it was Trojan.

I was just being paranoid.

"Hey, mate." He hugged tightly, and behind his shoulders I could see two young beautiful females. He pulled back and introduced, "This is Stella as you know," he pointed at the red haired girl, and then she pointed at the blond haired girl. "This is Jane," he winked.

Jane shook hands with me with a small smile and a giggle.

"You owe me, mate." Trojan chuckled. "Let's dance."

Everyone agreed, even me.

So before I tell about the dance—I should tell the important thing. I don't know how to dance. And when I stood at the court, and Jane just next to me, nearly close (or was trying to be close), grabbed my waist, and within a second pulled herself closer.

I could smell her perfume scent. It was rose.

She rounded her arms around my abdomen and kept her head down at my shoulder. The DJ had given a slow song. I also gripped her waist and with the footwork, I tried to be more flexible or so.

She didn't speak. Maybe she was lost in the dance. But I was lost in the missing Hunter. I was looking at everyone and assuming that maybe this is the Hunter or that is the Hunter...when my eye came upon Trojan!

Trojan was busy making out with Stella on the court instead of having an intimate dance.

Is he the Hunter?

The body language of that guy is as carefree as a...whatever. He cannot be a Hunter. And plus, he's too *human*.

I have some suspicion on Trojan but it is no use. Trojan is totally opposite to what a Hunter is.

After a while of dance, Trojan, Stella, Jane and I rested on the benches. Stella's silhouette had been making her feet pain, and she was moaning and telling Trojan how much pain she was in.

And Trojan was massaging her feet, comforting her. Whilst Jane and I sat awkwardly, trying to start some conversation. But our lips were not being opened at all.

Stella spoke, "See Dan—he's so handsome." She said to Jane.

Trojan didn't hear that and was busy helping her with the feet.

Jane nodded her head. "He's totally hot."

"You know what?" She whispered, but it was audible for me to hear. "He's calling me in his farmhouse."

She giggled as well as Jane also did.

Oh—so now Stella was ditching Trojan. But not only that, Dan was ditching Elena. I knew it. My heart was beating fast, and happiness came upon. Now I can have Elena—

Wait I'm thinking like Dan. I can't use this opportunity to get Elena.

Jane spoke in a low tone. "I've heard that Dan got a tattoo on his arm when he was almost a toddler. That's so brave of him!" She giggled.

"Yea..." she sniggered. "And this Greek boy has some random..."

Wait a minute!

I've heard that Dan got a tattoo on his arm when he was almost a toddler.

Tattoo...arm...mark...

Oh my gods...Dan is the Hunter!

Well it could be him. He has a hardboiled face. He's a cheater. He's tall and muscular. He doesn't care about anyone.

Yeah—Dan is a Hunter but evil according to me.

I looked to see Dan who was dancing. But then he got disturbed by his soccer friends. Ryan was whispering something to Dan which made him angry and made him look at me.

Elena also looked at me—tensed.

Dan left Elena on the court and came towards me with his soccer friends. Now what? What have I done now?

Have I broken another rule?

As he came nearer and nearer, my heart was thumping hard every second. My hand slipped inside my waist-coat and I had clutched my gun, so no one could see it.

But then, they turned their direction to Trojan and not me. I left my gun in the coat, and realized that Dan and his friends were actually not looking at me, but at Trojan who was behind me.

Jane and Stella just peered at him sheepishly and with a slight smile. Dan gave the smile back, and then turned to Trojan.

"Greek boy, we want you in private for a moment."

Trojan was in epiphany. He looked sideways at me, nervously. I had some pity on him. Dan took Trojan's collar, and took him inside the woods, which was little away from the court.

"Why Dan was angry at Trojan?" I asked Stella and Jane.

Stella answered in awe, "Ryan was my ex boyfriend. Maybe he disliked Trojan coming near me, huh."

Oh god! I sighed.

I looked at the court and saw Elena in anguish. I raced towards her on the floor. She looked down when I had approached. Elena just stamped her silhouette on the ground angrily.

"He always leaves me like this!" She mumbled.

"I'm sorry," I said.

"Oh you don't have to be," she looked up and I saw her red, dark lipstick.

Sudden warmth formed in my body. I don't know why. I looked at the woods. Dan and his gang with Trojan were visible. Dan was threatening Trojan and Trojan was scared to heck, listening carefully and not remarking back.

"Want to dance?"

Dan can take care of himself.

Maybe the winged guy was wrong. Maybe there was no danger. My watch isn't also beeping as Osiris had said before. Everything is fine.

Elena looked at me for a while as if studying me and thinking that can she trust this guy?

Then she just nodded with a slight smile. She kept her hands on my shoulder, and another hand on my palms, finger tinkering together. I kept my vacant hand on her hips.

She started moving her body around the floor, as well as I did. Well at least I have learnt to dance.

"So you work in Subway Station?"

"Yup—it's just part time." She replied.

"For…?"

"I want to be self employed. I don't want to be a burden on my family."

"Oh…so how's everything?"

"Not good, really," she said. "I think Dan is cheating me."

I just nodded.

"Isn't he?" She asked me.

I now had zipped my lips completely.

"Answer me, Damien." She paused. "I always have hope on you. You are not like his other friends. You are different. You are also close to me and not only too him. I expect a suitable answer."

I could see the pain in her eyes. She knew that Dan was cheating her. She was just confirming it from me.

I looked at the forest and saw that Dan and his friends with Trojan had disappeared. I narrowed my eyes.

BEEP! BEEP! ALERT!

There were some clicking noises from down. I left Elena's waist and moved away from her. She was surprised about what was happening to me. I looked down to see where the clicking voices were coming from…

Watch!

My digital watch showed red color on the screen, and said "ALERT! ALERT! DARK CREATURE ALERT!"

Oh my gods!

I ran!

I paced down the gap which was separated by two huge trees. I just ran, not thinking that where I was going.

I ended up coming in a place where some big bedrock was kept in slanting position. My boots had gone dirty as the soil had splattered.

And right now I was standing on mud.

The baldachins were letting the moonlight appear very mildly. I scampered into the deep forest, where the moonlight also didn't strike, and the darkness filled the vacant pace.

The screeching of the owl could be heard, and the rustling of the leaves gave me chills. At every second, I spurted, my heart galloped twice.

I was short of breath, and I stopped. I was between the trees, where an underbred of flowers was kept. I looked at my watch. I was near.

I need to move north.

I whisked further, until I saw the clearing. My face was now muddy as I had stepped inside a huge mud place before, and made my entire clothes dirty.

The clearing gave few striking lights which calmed my heart and my burning sensation. I moved forward but in now normal pace, trying to keep silent.

I heard some crackling voices which made my heart thump. I immediately grabbed my pistol, and moved forward.

The clearing was between two big coniferous trees,

which entangled their twigs to each other as if they were holding hands together.

I saw in front that there was an entire graveyard, filling the green enclosure. The tombstones were almost several and gave a touch of fright as the moonlight reflected on them.

As I moved further in crouching position, I saw Dan and his group with Trojan being held up. They were chuckling and laughing as Trojan shivered and shrieked.

Dan was pushing Trojan forward somewhere. I moved closer to get a good look and found that there was an entire pond with little water plants in them. The pond was dark and creepy, and gave me chills.

I switched off the beeping sound of my watch, as it was really annoying me, and stared at the bullying group.

"You mess with Stella, huh?" Ryan was yelling the most. "I will drown you to death."

Dan pushed Ryan back, and gave a fierce look. "Wait— let me handle his business." He gave a dangerous, looking smile and spoke. "You know this pond. This pond was once a graveyard itself. Many corpses were drowned here. The famous murder of Billy the Butcher was done here. He was drowned and his body was never found."

Okay, now they were scaring a skunk out of me.

Dan was trying to push Trojan inside the pond. Now they have broken the limits of bullying.

I moved forward, out of the clearing, into the lichgate which was crafted and designed like a huge hut, with a roof symbolizing the walking dead.

The little green sprouts of leaves were growing on the large enclosure, and covered the most of the tombstones. There was a stone hinged path which reached the pond and where the group stood with Trojan.

I kept my gun in the holster back, so I could persuade Dan and his friends to leave Trojan alone.

"Hey…" I said loudly.

Dan and his little group looked back at me. Everyone's eye shined. "What are you doing here, new bee?"

I walked forward. "What are you doing guys? This is insane. Leave the Greek boy alone and let's party, huh?" I tried to be cheerful.

Dan smiled…and unbelievably he was having…

Fangs!

"Shit," I muttered.

Everyone in the group started smiling. And well, everyone had the freaking fangs instead of their teeth. Their pupils turned purple and their finger nails turned long.

Now I am dealing with Vampires—oh no worries!

So my assumption that Dan was a Hunter—was wrong.

Dan snouted, "Don't interfere in our matters, Damien Black! We want this boy only…" he pointed at Trojan.

I took my gun out, and said "And why do you want him? Because he is new fresh blood."

"So you are a Hunter too." Dan laughed fiercely. "Now my fellow beings, we have two preys to catch."

His skin, pale and chalk white, and his hands, bloodless and thorny.

"What do you mean by 'Too'?"

"The Greek boy is also a Hunter!"

My hands were shaking. First, because I just got to know that Trojan was himself a Hunter—second, the mist started spreading across the graveyard, and towards the broken cathedral.

The moon was now shading away due to the atmospheric changes. The skies were turned fallow and gloomy and foggy as if someone was playing with the weather.

The obscure vampires were also startled when this happened. Trojan was laid on the tenebrous grass, and watching in an unhinged manner.

The ground started shaking and I remembered the words what that angel said:

The dead will rise!

I looked down.

I was standing near a tombstone, on the grave. Something got a hold of my leg, something really strong. I looked down to see the leg catcher and found an arm.

I shot the arm and collapsed backwards on the grass. The arm broke, but then the elbow sprouted from the ground. It broke the graves marble covering and made himself rise up on the ground.

He was wearing an American hat, with a navy uniform on himself. He was having a huge sheath in his hand from which he took out the saber. His face was fleshy, bare, with bones being visible, and his top notch eyes half portaging out of his socket.

He yelled like a Hyena, and clashed his saber towards me, but I rolled over at the exact timing.

I immediately stood up and shot the silver bullet on the zombie's head. I looked at Ryan who had hustled Trojan on his back to take him away.

I shot him too—at his heart, which made him decompose and disappear in ashes.

Dan squawked in anger and ran towards me with Phil, Chris and Tom on the sides.

I saw Trojan helping himself up on his feet but he was helpless as two zombies were approaching him. He was defending himself by a pen.

I ran forward, away from the vampire group, keeping my pace.

POP!

One more zombie came in front, and I slid down the grass. I shot numerous bullets without even seeing and found that I had killed two zombies who were trying to kill me, and I even shot Chris.

I took my dagger out, and pressed the green button to make it form the shape of a sword. Tom and Phil attacked me from the back whilst Dan did it from the front.

Phil caught my one arm and Tom caught another. Dan came forward towards me. His fangs growing larger — I saw at the back, the zombies were increasing rapidly, breaking themselves from the tombs.

"You are going to die, Hunter!" He paused as he touched my collarbone softly. "I liked you as a human. But I never expected that you would be a Hunter. Hunters have extinct us around the globe. We will take revenge. For many days, we were trying to find a Hunter but then we saw Trojan. We could smell his innocent blood. He was a Hunter. We planned out everything. But we started enjoying our lives here and forgot our real duty."

"Who gave you this duty?" I demanded.

"Our Creator," he hissed.

CLANK!

A rock hit Dan's head, which distracted Phil and Tom. I immediately kicked Dan's stomach, and bellowed my elbows back at the two bully vampires who collapsed.

I shot the three Vampires down. I could see Dan's tattoo in his transparent white shirt (as his coat had been removed before). It was a tattoo of a dragon.

I looked at the rock thrower and saw Elena standing, baffled, amazed and full of fright. Her dress was muddy and her make-up had worn off.

We stayed silent for a moment when Trojan shouted, "Someone help, please!"

Elena and I looked at Trojan. He was defending himself by a boulder. Zombies with crooked backs, and colored uniforms were attacking Trojan with their spears and swords.

Elena rushed towards me, and asked "You have a lot to explain, Mr."

I gave a weak nod.

We ran towards Trojan. At the time, I was thinking that maybe I should call Osiris and Athena, but there was no time. I had switched off my watch before (remember!).

I handed Elena the sword, and I took the gun. Zombies were erupting like small bubble gums from the graves, and I was shooting them. Some bullets were going elsewhere whilst some blasted their brains and their hearts off.

To my surprise, Elena was slicing the zombies nicely and tidily with my sword. It felt as if she was an expert in this all.

Is she also a Hunter?

Oh no...not one more.

I was groaning numbly.

Elena stabbed the sword inside the zombies who were trying to kill Trojan.

"You fine?" I asked Trojan.

"You have a lot to explain." Trojan clenched his teeth.

The ground started shaking again. We all looked back, and saw the biggest zombie protruding himself out of the longest grave.

The zombie was almost seven feet tall, with loose eyes, and fleshy skin. His hair was springing up, and his forehead was already decomposed by some worms that were still eating his brain. He was in a military dress with his green uniform dirty and covered with soil.

"Ah..."

"Well, haven't you heard the saying: When the dead will

walk, the living will fill the coffins?" I tried to make them cheer up.

They frowned at me.

"What next?" Elena asked. "Get eaten by this monster which somehow I thought existed in some fantasy land like Alice in the Wonderland."

"A zombie isn't a fantasy character, for dead sake." Trojan argued. "They somehow relate to reality."

"Well the reality is here, eh?" I grinned.

The zombie moved forward, clearing the mist which was in the midst. I shot some bullets at his chest, but that wasn't working. He just walked slowly and steadily as if he has all the time in the world.

I was pretty scared right now. My hands were shaking. I didn't know what to do. I had no idea.

I turned my face to ask Elena and Trojan about the plan but I could see only Elena, who just stared at the zombie in unbelievable expression.

Where was Trojan?

"Help…help!"Someone yelled.

Elena and I turned our faces to see Trojan being drowned inside the pond. But not because Trojan wasn't a swimmer, but because fleshy zombie arms were catching him down.

"Distract that monster, I'll rescue Trojan." I said to Elena.

She weakly nodded.

I jumped inside the black, dark water which was quite ominous. The pond wasn't a small pond. It was severely deep and I could not feel my feet on ground.

Trojan was immediately grabbed down inside the water. I inhaled lot of breath, and took a dip inside the water.

I opened my eyes, and saw the green vegetation which was seven feet down. I looked for Trojan, and finally caught his sight.

Little way further, he was carried down at the depths

by two zombies. I swam forward. As I had a gun in my hand, there was no use of shooting, since the velocity of the bullet would be very slow.

I saw Trojan struggling in the black water, crying and opening his mouth so he could feel air but only water galloped inside.

I swam further, and then kicked one of the zombies on the face, breaking his jaw and separating it from his head. Then with the hilt of my gun, I knocked off the other zombie who was holding Trojan's left arm.

Trojan pointed his finger at the back. I looked back, and saw a zombie swimming towards me. He was having a butcher's knife in his hand.

So—the Billy the Butcher is dead but remains undead—that is not cool.

He was fat and was wearing an apron which floating along with his obese body. He threw his knife towards me.

I deflected it by my gun's hilt.

I took Trojan's hand, and screeched him down in the deep. Billy the Butcher was confused of where we went, and started searching down.

My lungs were now exhausted and I felt string of burning sensation in my body.

Billy the Butcher turned his face, and at that exact time, I aimed my gun at his head, and I knew the velocity would not be slow now.

BOOM!

The sound was very mild, but the effect was massive. I saw Billy's head being smashed, and scattered, with his brains and eyes and nerves swinging in the black water.

We came to the surface, and took a breath of relief.

I saw Elena being cuffed on her neck by the seven foot zombie. From the pond only I shot some bullets which somehow (I really didn't aim) hit him numerously and made him unconscious.

Elena fell with him down, and sighed happily.

We came back to the grass area, and took deep panting breaths until we could talk. Elena was also having a hard time. Her red dress was now torn till her thighs, and her face was all soiled and muddy, her hair was all sticky and slimy, and surprisingly she didn't care.

Trojan smiled spontaneously, his eyes all troubled and weak, whispered: "The good news is we get marvelous opportunity to see Elena Sanchez legs."

I chuckled.

Elena's back was on the tombstone, and her legs were sprawled on the grave. She was panting and taking breaths with my sword being rested on her side.

A hand suddenly crept out of the grave...oh shit not again!

She yelled.

She immediately took the sword and slaughtered the hand.

"We must go...fast!"

I came on my feet and declared. "We can't go. The zombies are just injured. We haven't killed them yet. We must find their last possessions."

Elena walked towards me, and gave an eye to eye expression. "What the heck do you mean? Our town would be the 'Night of the Living Dead' soon?"

"If we don't find their possessions."

Trojan also came up on his feet. "And what kind of possessions you are talking about?"

"Whenever a corpse is buried in a graveyard, one of the materials from their life is kept as a relic inside the crypt of the cathedral..." I pointed at the small church and continued. "These become their last possessions which make them undead until those possessions aren't burnt soon."

"And till how much time is left to wake up?" Elena asked.

"Soon," I gave a scared expression.

Trojan blistered his water soaked shirt, and said, "Okay, so we have to find their possessions which are according to you in the crypt of the cathedral. So what are we waiting for?"

Elena nodded her head. "He's right. And after the town saving and all, Damien—I need to have the 'talk' and you strictly know what I mean."

I was more panicked from Elena than the zombies who were going to wake up soon.

We rushed towards the church, which was a small build house type. We entered the building, and saw the pavilion and the row seats; the bishop's seat was at the top, near the ceiling.

The walls were painted cream colored, and there was a huge fallen photograph embroidered on the multi colored glass.

But the place was half broken, entire dirty with dust spiraling like spiders, and cobwebs were formed creating discomfort here. The smell was awful even, as if there was a sewer problem nearby and the entire fragrance was closed inside.

We found the staircases under the semicircular recess covered with a dome which led us down at a small enclosed chamber. The place was full of smoke and dust, which surrounded the ceilings, the walls and the ground.

There was a carpet which was much stained (and showed that it had been hundreds of years who hadn't stopped by here), half torn and half misled to some other path.

There was a huge cabinet which joined the wall, made of wood, and was frameless. The box shaped piece of furniture was mounted by a gold lock.

I shot the lock, and opened the wooden cabinet. There were twenty or so relics of the deceased people, capped inside big caskets of jars.

"They are coming!"

Yes and they were. The irritating, moaning voices were becoming audible every minute.

We scattered all the relics down at the ground when Trojan asked, "Why hasn't someone taken these relics away?"

"This is an independent church. The burial is not taken place officially and so, the caretaker only buries the corpse, and takes away one of the possession, keeps it in these kinds of jars. I know it's creepy but it's a fact."

"But after deceased decomposed span…why have they waken just now?"

"They must be summoned by someone or been conducted to walk the streets of Earth…" Azazel is the culprit.

I know it's Azazel. Osiris had told me about him. He's trying to kill every Hunter around the globe so he wouldn't have problems with them in the future.

"Now how would we burn them?" Elena asked, trying to search something which can ignite a fire.

I showed my gun.

"I can switch my Beretta to different sorts of varieties. It's magical." I commanded to the Beretta. "Incendiary Ammunition!"

Something clicked in the Beretta. I aimed at the relics. Elena saw that the zombies had entered the chamber and were moving towards them.

BOOM!

I shot.

The bullet volcanically hit the relics, and it produced a low, murmuring spark which created enkindled light.

The relics were in flames.

The zombies, coming to eat our brains, were now into ashes.

"We saved the night!" Trojan jumped in the air. "You know what guys," he turned to Elena and me with a large grin of satisfaction on his face and continued. "We should be the Zombie Busters much like Ghostbusters, huh?"

Elena and I confusingly narrowed our eyes. Elena snorted, "In your dreams. I did this just one time. Now I feel little...EWWW!" She started hopping on the carpet. "That was just warrior hibernation. Now I'm back to what I am really."

"A piggy attitude chick," Trojan mumbled.

The good thing was that Elena didn't listen to what Trojan said, but the bad thing was that Elena and Trojan came up to me and said, "You have lots to explain."

I took Trojan and Elena with me towards the dance floor, which now was emptied. Then we left for home. I first escorted Elena till she reached her home and promised her that I would explain tomorrow at her house. Then I took Trojan to his house, and told him to come to my haunted mansion after school so I could make him meet Osiris, we could discuss about all this stuff which is going on (and which is new for him in another words, fascinating).

"I met the Hunter." I was undressing myself in my room, when I said those words to Athena.

She was wagging her tail, and which purely indicated that she was happy. "Who was it?"

"Of course Trojan—I never expected that. He was just—whoops—and he's a Hunter. I even saw his mark. He just had the Pentagon tattoo, I wonder why."

Yea and what was it !

Chapter - 9

The Black Skull

As I was escorting Trojan back at his home, I asked him to show his hand. He did and I saw his mark. It was different from mine. That was puzzling.

"He's from a Greek Legion, Damien." Athena said. "Every Legion has their own ways of showing marks. Maybe they just preferred a Pentagon."

"But why Pentagon only, why that star is on a Hunters hand?"

"It signified difference from other humans, Damien, anyhow. Osiris is really proud of you. But you must now elude in your mind that when you are going to be attacked by some zombies, you must inform us before."

"I wanted to defeat them by myself. I am a professional now. And plus Elena also helped me killing most of the zombies."

"Hmmm…and what about the bullies…"

I interrupted. "They were unexpected. They turned into Vampires. They said their kind is becoming extinct."

"Those Vampires aren't from Underworld. They are not under Azazel. But as for the zombies—Azazel was behind it. He was striking two at one time. You and Trojan,"

I nodded my head. "But what should we do now?"

"We will wait."

Another voice had spoken and it was Osiris.

Osiris was leaning on the patent of the door, with his arms folded on his chest, and his grey hair grizzled on the left. He added, "We do not have any other home now. We will wait here until I'll find more about the other Hunters location."

"And what about the skull, Osiris," Athena asked, with her head tilted on the right. "Did you locate it?"

"No, but I have a feeling that it's not protected."

"You know what will happen if it goes in the wrong hands." Athena spoke.

"Hmmm…I'm trying to find." He pressed his lips, and then left my room.

"What about the skull?" I asked.

"The Black Skull, Damien—I hope you remember, I had recalled about it before, when you were small."

"The skull which could bring world at end!"

Athena nodded. "Anyways, you should not get into this mess. But you must take care about the—you know—Elena thing. She knows our secret now. She has to confide or forget." She winked.

I knew what she meant. Forgetting Potion created specially by Osiris. We use most of that potion on humans who knows our secret.

"I'm meeting her tomorrow."

"You should better." Athena's eyes were bloodshot red, giving a glimmer of horror. "We don't want anyone, Damien, to interfere in this secret affair. If you really care about this girl, I should warn you—she's *already* in trouble."

The next day was quite quirky and embarrassing. When I went to the school, I saw that no one even thought where

Dan and his group had gone. Instead, one more group of bullies had formed, and everyone was terrorized by them now (I hope they aren't Vampires).

I even saw Trojan and Elena. Trojan greeted me normally as if yesterday was nothing to him. He was good at hiding his mental tension. But well, he was Trojan, and he started asking questions like:

"Hey man, who are we going to slaughter today? Zombies again," and then he laughed.

Then in Moral Education class (in which we were studying about demons), he asked me, "we would be like...like...Sam and Dean Winchester in *Supernatural* series, eh? We would beat the crap out of demons and monsters, eh? Eh?"

I didn't answer his stupid questions. Well because of three reasons:

First—when I learnt about these Hunter stuff and these monsters that live on Earth unaware by humans from Osiris, I also acted the exact same (maybe more) and asked stupid questions. So I bear whatever heck he was saying, just realizing how Osiris would be handling me when I was acting the same like Trojan?

Second—well because, Osiris had conducted me that he will guide Trojan well enough than me!

Third—Ah...uh...there's no third reason.

So I was not only pissed off from Trojan but from Elena also. She was ignoring me all day. She wasn't even looking at me, and she didn't even show that I existed in this world (like when I had that dream...)

Then it hit me!

The dream—that wicked, vivid, crazy dream!

That dream in which an angel sort of guy approached me and told, I will be attacked by the dead (zombies in another words), and that happened.

He was the helper.

He had helped.

If I didn't know about the dead rising, I would have never rescued Trojan—I would have never found out that Dan and his group were actually from a vampire clan.

He had helped (except that he hadn't told me about Dan) but still, he did, he did help.

If he can tell the dangers which will come in the future, it would be like—like I watch future but I consult with someone without cost (that's cool).

I need to see that guy again. I am just scared that if I will not find him, then what will I be? Just a loser!

Someone threw a rolled parchment at me. I unrolled it, and read it in my mind:

Meet me at my house at night around 10. I think you know where my house is. But come through the window. If you are really a superman I want to see how you jump to one storey building.

I tore off the paper and kept it inside my black jacket. I sighed. Well—I'm going to have a night date with Elena now. Great!

After the school, I took Trojan with me to my haunted mansion, where Athena was sitting, under the terrace roof.

Athena said with a smile as she waged her tail, "Oh hello, you must be Trojan?"

Trojan looked at me with a stunned expression. He was so stunned that he almost had fainted but fortunately he didn't. "Oh my gods—what now… a talking mice!"

We made Trojan sit in the living room, on the sofas where a bright sheet of light dropped through the mourning window. The ceilings were dreaded more than ever, and the plaster was dripping from the edges.

The living room was connected to the ground floor bedrooms, and even the portable kitchen where Peter was working and bringing coffee for us (especially for Trojan as he would be needing lots of caffeine).

Osiris came in his most usual dress. His favored long double breasted overcoat, slung down till his dark purple pants. His waistcoat having all the potions studded on it and even the white collared shirt which now over rounded at the overcoat's collar!

He had trimmed his French beard, and his hair was now dyed, and looked more gleaming than before. He looked different or so I thought.

Osiris sat on the main couch which looked much like a throne but instead had soft cushioned arms instead of brass dragon designated arm.

Osiris had a beaming expression today (as he was the first time when he told me all about this stuff), He said in the most polite and calm way:

"Trojan you are different."

Trojan was being childish. He started clapping hands, and then suddenly stopped and said. "Oh ho…am I Harry Potter? I can wear those round spectacles you want."

"No, no, no," Osiris wavered off. "You are not Harry Potter or Percy Jackson or even another some guy? You are a Hunter."

"And what are these Hunters mate?"

Oh he started his pirate talk again!

I interrupted the conversation of Osiris and Trojan and asked, "You mean he does not know that he's a Hunter?" I asked Osiris.

"Well, some don't. He wouldn't have gotten any education about the kindred of Hunters from anyone."

"Shouldn't he be killed by them now?"

"Well when a Hunter does not know about his own well

being, it is that time, he is considered as a human. So the monsters do not think him as a threat or possibly they cannot get him as he had adapted himself as a human."

I kept myself back on the couch and listened to the description what Osiris said.

He told everything to Trojan about Hunters (except their unknown origin history), about their ways of living, about their motives. He also told about the Hunters law:

1) Hunters shall not disclose their identity with any human.
2) Hunters cannot fall in love.
3) Hunters cannot mix their normal life with their hunter life.
4) Hunters cannot turn themselves to the Underworld.
5) Hunters cannot hurt a human.
6) Hunters must take a pledge of saving humanity.

Then well, he told about Underworld to Trojan. Trojan started shivering after hearing the story. Osiris explained that all the dead souls, ghouls, demons, vampires, werewolves and other Dark Creatures are in that parallel world who come on Earth through a portal called the Cave. Their only entry and exits is the Cave. He also told about the Black Skull:

"The Black Skull history is actually unknown. Some say that it has a past which can ruin the future. But all I and Athena know is that the Black Skull is actually the most powerful artifact in the entire universe. Well because..." Osiris gave a look at Athena just to make sure about the thing. Athena nodded her head, with her eye lids slightly down in apprehension. "Because it can raise Lucifer."

I was baffled. I was never told about Lucifer. Even Trojan was speechless for a moment, with his jaw falling down, and drool dripping from his mouth.

The lamps which hung on every corner of the wall flickered simultaneously due to electric shortage but our minds were too clocked with confusion that we didn't care about the lamps.

"I'm not much a Catholic, but are you talking about the Fallen Angel?"

"No!" Osiris shook his head and we despaired with relief. "Actually he's worse than the Bible Lucifer!"

"What?"

"Oh yes...according to the ancient scriptures, it is said that he is omniscient and has the power of virtual omnipotence."

We squeaked miserably.

Osiris hesitated. "But the good part is, the Black Skull can also destroy the portal which can stop the Dark Creatures to come on Earth if we practice the right ritual on it."

Trojan nodded his head in approval. He saw Peter coming with a tray. Trojan immediately took the coffee and gulped it in one go. Then watched Peter's green disfigured face and grimed. Peter lowered his head and went away back in the kitchen to make the supper.

"This isn't cool, mate." He said to me.

"I told you."

"What if the Lucifer rises?" He asked Osiris.

"The world will end." He got his reply.

Trojan's adrenaline had now become rapid. I could make out through his thumping heart, and his shivering body. His eyes were still and frozen.

"What about me?"

"You will stay with your foster parents..."

"My parents aren't my real parents?"

"Of course they aren't. They have adopted you." Osiris replied. "I researched before. I know it's hard on you but understand the fact. You have to take it in a Hunter way like Damien did. You have a destiny. You have a destiny to save humanity if any crisis occurs."

His eyes had become oval. "So...what should we do now? What we will do now?" He changed the topic as he was hurt.

"I am trying to locate the Black Skull. It is impossible. I also haven't got any news that Azazel is trying to take the Black Skull which is...good news. So we have to wait until something, about Black Skull comes upon or about another surviving Hunter like you."

Trojan and I came out of my haunted mansion with Athena on my side. He said to me, "My parents were killed in a war." Osiris had told him that.

"Hunters don't have a long life as they are trying to battle for humanity." I said. "My parents were also killed. So you shouldn't feel bad. They died with honor. And they want you to follow the legacy."

He embraced me tightly and I did him back. It felt good that someone just like me could understand the same pain which I went through. Trojan was like me. He was right...as he had told me before:

I feel as if I'm like you.

He was speaking honestly like me.

He pulled back, and smiled warmly. "You know what— I've a feeling that we will have a long friendship on the road, mate."

And he has started his pirate talk again. Honestly speaking—I was getting used to it.

"We will dude, we will." I gestured.

Chapter - 10

The Night of Love

It was 10, and I was standing at the backyard of Elena's house. Her parents hadn't noticed my incoming. I was too quick and too fast (the door to the backyard was open).

There was a small pond in that yard with a huge bushy trees surrounded by bushes itself. I climbed through the twigs and approached the upper branches.

Then, I jumped to the foliage, and sat on the crown of the green leaves which overlooked the house. The windows were representing huge light on me.

Then they were opened.

I saw Elena standing and calling me out. I jumped towards the window panel (I was almost going to fall), and reached up to her room.

Her room was locked from inside.

I looked around the view of room and then realized something. It was dull. It was amazingly, unpredictably dull and boring.

The ceilings were dark brown, the walls were painted dark blue, and the carpet was fluffy soft and black in color. Her bed sheets were scattered along the rug on the ground, her pillows were thrown near the cabinet, and the TV was on.

The room didn't signify Elena Sanchez at all.

I wanted to ask, "Who are you really?" But that would be rude. So I began the conversation with, "What about you?"

Elena was in her normal, dress up pajamas (if you call a knees up shorts and a shoulder less top a pajama), white slippers. Her hair was tied in a ponytail and some freckles fell on her creased forehead.

She was looking amazing, but that wasn't what she was really—according to the room.

"This is real Elena, Damien." He pointed at the rough, boy type room. "What I am in school—that's just a part which Dan had made me into." She paused, giving a smirk, but it was a sad, smirk. "I'm actually an introvert, no makeup, no fashionable dress girl. I hated make up actually."

I lifted my brows. Split personality, I thought.

"My father had trained me to be an army girl the side you have seen at the cemetery. I hated those soft toys and those temporary make up and dresses. But then I met Dan. He was great at first. He didn't like of who I was. He changed me completely into this..." she pointed her dress. "Now my pajamas are also so revealing."

"Your father didn't say anything?"

"My father died a year ago in a car crash. After that only I met Dan." She nodded her head. "But then you came. And after that cemetery thing, I realized that I was some Barbie doll before. You had made me like this. I want to thank you."

And yes, you are thanking me by ignoring me in the school. Whoa.

I didn't say that. It would be rude towards her. "I don't want to scatter you inside this. So…" I ruffled my hand inside my black waistcoat and took out a bottle which Osiris had given me. "Here…drink this potion and concentrate to forget what had happened at the cemetery."

She took the potion in her hand, and looked at it for a while, as if she was examining it, which actually she was contemplating.

She sat on her bed. Opened up the cap of bottle, and put the bottle towards her mouth—

"Stop," I said.

She did.

Her eyes were blank as a hole.

"Listen I want to tell you something before you drink this potion. I want to tell you who I am really…which would be a relief for me because I'm disclosing my identity to a human." I added. "You will forget it eventually but you must know who I really am."

And so I began.

I told her everything about Hunters, Osiris, and Athena, about the Dark Creatures, about Azazel about Lucifer, the Black Skull, and even about the winged man (I don't know why I told her about it).

"You saw an angel in your dream?"

"I suppose." I answered. "He told me once about the future. He also told that Osiris holds a secret which can change my life."

"That's mysterious," Elena sniggered. "Haven't you seen in ancient scriptures of Hunter theology that who he is…?"

That's a good idea—I'm such a dork. But I just shook my head negatively.

"I just want to…you know…remove burden from my chest. It felt good that I can share these things to a girl…I like." And it slipped off.

I like!

Skunk!

I was sitting down at the carpet, and she was on the bed—looking blankly at me as if I spoke Spanish to her. I bit my tongue. I didn't want her to know about the likeness towards her.

"Can you...you know...when you drink this potion, can you concentrate on forgetting that point also..."

And it happened.

She jumped towards me and kissed me, making me fall on my back with her. Her fingers rolled in my black hair, and her legs had wrapped around my waist. Her mouth was inside mine, and well—I do not know how to describe—because the kiss was indescribable with some tongue movements and all.

"I love you," she sighed.

"Why haven't you told me before?" I was now having the potion. I didn't want her to forget that she loved me, so just in case I kept it by my side.

We were on the bed, and she was blushing totally. "I was scared. First it was Dan; well I found out that he was an evil vampire. Second, I got to know that you weren't human. I don't want to love a person who has responsibilities. I don't want to be part of that person who I can distract."

Nice explanations.

"Aren't you over Dan?"

"Yes I am. He was not my type. Well as for you," she cuddled my cheeks. "You were amazing. You were love at first sight."

"Believe it or not, the same was with me—but I could not understand that they were real affections or some sort."

She chortled and took my hand. "So my previous boy friend was a vampire and my present boyfriend is a Hunter. I have very good strings of variety boyfriends."

I chuckled.

But as I looked at the happy face, who stared back at me, I just remembered one thing that time:

Hunters cannot fall in love with humans.

Chapter - 11

The Warning
By The Winged Dude

It was few days later when I had the dream…

I was back at the same dream where the winged guy had come upon. But this time, I wasn't standing near the oak tree or the boulders, I was in the meadow where the trees and the flowers were present and giving low mumblings.

"Isn't it beautiful, Damien?" A calm voice spoke.

I immediately turned, and saw…

No one!

Oh—so now I'm listening voices.

I looked around the field, and the grassland which ended at the woods. I even looked at the large coniferous, marsh up trees.

"You haven't answered me, Damien?"

"I prefer seeing you first and then answering." I replied loudly.

"Look up then."

I did.

So he was there. The black wing guy!

He was in mid air, almost twelve feet above me, walking as if there was an invisible bridge formed. But what I didn't notice that he was flapping his wings.

The birds were roaming around him, and he was smiling at them, playing with them.

"I love this place...well because...this is my dream." I said to him.

He laughed.

"Oh...a chucky boy, aren't you?"

He was talking to me as if I'm nine year old guy.

"I want to talk to you...so..." He lifted his hands up, making me also lift up automatically in the air.

I finally came in the air, just next to him, and saw that my feet were touching something hard. I looked down to see on what I was standing now and found a cloud under my feet, lifting me up.

"Mystical, isn't it?" He smiled. "Damien. I have a purpose here..."

I touched the cloud. It was spongy and smoky.

"Damien...Damien...Damien...are you listening to me?" He was blabbering but I was busy playing with the cloud. "This is important Damien." He shook my shoulders.

"Yea...uh...ah..." I replied.

The angel sighed.

"So...was my prediction right?" He asked me kindly, whilst he caught a bird, cuffed it inside his palms and patted the bird's head.

"Uh...yea at one end," I answered. "Vampires also attacked me, you know. But about the dead raising, oh yea, the zombies just—you know—jumped from the grave."

The winged guy gave a cold look. "You teenagers talk like so casually to everyone...?"

"Uh…" I thought for a moment. "Uh…yes. Well actually, a teenager different like me, if sees a guy with wings particularly in black is controlling their dreams, they really — you know — talk like this."

"Every time like this…"

"Well it is upon a nature of that teenager."

"And how's your nature?"

"Why are you asking me about my nature?"

"Well because you're talking style is really irritating me, Damien." The guy literally said those words.

I looked around the view, trying to be casual about the conversation. Then he broke the silence, and said, "Do not tell about me to anyone."

"And why is that?"

The winged dude touched my forehead, and said, "I am a Helper which comes in dreams of Hunters. But if they disclose my identity, I will erase from your memory and you will never be able to know the future."

I changed the topic.

"Are you the medium who connected me to my past when I saw my dad being killed by Grim Reaper?"

"Yes, Damien. I had connected you to that." He nodded his head.

"So why have you come just now to me?" I asked. "Why not before — I had many dangerous expeditions before arriving in South County. You could warn me many times."

The winged dude spoke, "Well, actually Damien — everything happens according to Time. I came at the right time, and I will tell you at the right time eventually."

"So let me guess — you have nothing to say right now and that is why you are just talking about this stuff."

"Wow…where did you learn that?"

"Have you ever heard the name — Internet?"

The wing dude shook his head blankly, but then cleared

his thoughts and said. "Listen, I have come here to warn you to not tell about me to anyone. Problems and misconceptions will be created. It is good, if everything is going all right."

"Okay as you say. But do you know anything about the Black Skull?" I had tilted my body, near to the edge of the combed cloud.

He narrowed his eyes, scratched his skin, as if trying to find some excuse, and spoke. "Damien, I do not know anything about it. But what I know is that you are stuffing inside this all non sense. You must free yourself and be with Elena..." I don't know how he knew about Elena but still I let him continue his speech. "You have to experience humanity, Damien. When you found out that Elena loves you back, how did you feel?"

That thing really hit me.

He was right.

When I realized that Elena really likes me, I actually felt good. I had never felt that way. I was always squeezed between Athena and Osiris, or between different creatures. But now, as I stood on a floating cloud (I still don't know how that winged dude used that cloud to lift me up) I smiled.

I felt *human* when I was with Elena.

"Think wisely, Damien." He smiled. "Osiris has secrets about...your father, Damien. We will meet soon..."

I woke up!

Chapter - 12

More About The Winged Dude

The next week after that dream was actually a blur. I was having the best time ever, but all I could hear and see: *Osiris knows secrets about your father, Damien.*

What secrets?

What about my father?

I can't even ask Osiris that *hey Osiris, I just got hold of this winged dude; he told me that you hold a powerful secret about my father. Would you mind telling me?*

Plus, if I'll even ask Osiris, I can't mention the winged dude then. It would create misconceptions. As he had said to me—and I need him if anything comes further.

So what I did was something opposite…

Trojan had arrived at my haunted mansion. He was settling on the sofa, when I brought him up from the couch and made him rush into the library where Osiris keeps all his books, scriptures and parchments which were important since decades ago.

Athena had followed me. I didn't have problems with her as I could trust her thoroughly. She would never tell my mischievous plans to Osiris until it turns really, really bad for example raising the band of demons or so.

We entered the small study room of his (remember, he hates his materials to be touched which are from the study room), and made our self accompanied.

"What are we finding, Damien?"

Trojan and I looked around the bundle of sheets, books, folders kept everywhere in the room, occupying most the vacant space. There was a dim light in the small room due to stable lamp on the study table.

"More about the helper."

"Helper...?" Trojan quizzed.

Athena snorted. "You mean the helper which helps Hunters in bad times."

I nodded my head.

Athena started to make his search for the Aid Master. She jumped at the top shelf where most of the sheets and folders were kept, with her teeth, brought on the ground. Her paws turned the pages of a folder, and then in sustenance, she said "Here it is."

Trojan and I turned to look at Athena's paw which was indicating a passage.

I picked it up, while Athena spoke, "The helper was known as Dogma. Dogma was actually the last among his race which was known as the Vultures. The Vultures are the creatures who devote their lives for safety of Hunters as they possess different sorts of power which are useful."

The same lines which Athena had said were written in that message.

"Dogma helped many Hunters during the Civil War, World War 2 and even Vietnam War."

Trojan scratched his head at that time.

So this is the guy. So this is the one who's helping me. This guy was a good guy. I can trust him.

"What was all that about?" Trojan asked me the next day.

I knew what he was talking about. His mind works a little late. So when he asked this question, I really didn't know what to answer. I can't tell him about the winged dude.

"Uh...well I heard Osiris talking about him. So you know, I just whooped up to see that it was. Just curious, you know."

And plus I remembered that Elena also knows about Dogma. I had told her before. But well I told her before he told me not to tell anyone. So technically it's not my fault.

I looked around the lighted corridor, and saw a bunch of kids rambling and rumbling all around. I saw a group of bullies raided by Aaron some new fresh bully now. He was short and grumpy like a Dwarf.

Elena came up to me with a smile. She was not wearing fashionable clothes anymore. She looked nice the way as she wore normal, average looking clothes.

She hugged me.

Trojan spoke, "So...Elena...didn't you feel bad about Dan?"

I eyed to him. He's starting a pitiful conversation.

"Who's Dan?" She asked, puzzled.

Trojan looked at me in amusement. "Dan...the big guy with broad shoulders and huge curly hair, you don't remember?"

"Nope."

I waved at Trojan to stop, and mouthed "Will tell later on." I turned to Elena who was confused a lot. "Your class has started." She gave a paused nod, kissed me, and by touching her forehead in confusion went towards her class.

I punched Trojan!

Trojan spoke, "What was that all about?"

"Humans lose the memory of a Dark Creature who dies." I smiled. "There are so many wars between Underworld and the Hunters on Earth. Many humans see that war, and run away from it, but then they forget about it, as if nothing ever happened."

"Why is that?"

"Humans consciousness is always triggered when it comes to magic, Greek boy." I said. "Anyhow, what is Osiris teaching you?"

We were going towards our class.

"About the Dark Creatures defiance—Vampires repel to garlic." He said it as if it was such a big thing. "Nowadays I'm eating only garlic."

"But Vampires do not only attack humans...Werewolves, shape shifters, basilisk, serpent— anyone can just jump at you and catch you."

"I'm a Greek—Zeus is with me." He winked, and then we went inside the class.

Chapter - 13

The Days to Remember

The next few days with me was really cool and romantic. Trojan and I dwelt at my place after school, and dueled together. And whoever won would get a secret gift (which was nothing and we made the secret gift just for the heck).

Later on, at nights, without telling Osiris and Athena (Athena caught me several times but she didn't inform Osiris about it or did she?) I sneaked out and went to Elena's house where I spent time alone.

Her mother usually doesn't come in Elena's room as she minds her privacy. Elena would always wait for me, near the window, while she hears the screeching of an owl.

I usually came up to her, and we would end up having a quite good time. It was really difficult for me to jump from the large tree which ended near her window. So Elena kept a long rope which writher down the house. And as my grip was strong, I could easily pull myself up and when I come at the window, I kiss her unexpectedly and she giggles and slaps me on the shoulders.

For several weeks, we never slept in the night as we thought that it would be wasting time. I needed sleep, and sometimes as she describes her family history, I take a nap—not listening to her. When she realizes that I have slept, she hits me and we end up cuddling.

I really didn't have a clue in these weeks that this connection between me and Elena is true or just infatuation?

During the classes also, I start mesmerizing that what really love is and what infatuation is? But I always kept in my heart that it was love, and it was plain, romantic love (I was looking at the affirmative side).

And slowly, gradually the correlation between me and her increased, which resulted me in becoming too protective for her. Not to forget that when she is with me that means she is with danger. The Dark Creatures roam on Earth and want to kill me, so Elena who's always with me, could also get hurt somehow.

Osiris didn't know anything about Elena-Damien's love, and I wanted to keep it that way. Athena was trustworthy, but still I feared that she can tell Osiris everything, but as expected she never did. I always shared problems with Athena (Trojan was not experienced in love and Osiris hated love), because I felt good.

Athena was understandable and nodded her head, listening to my boring talks. She even guided me saying, "You can ardor a human, but you must understand that you are creating her life suicidal."

Some part of me wanted to protest on those words, but some part of me knew that Athena was right. I was like a wild sheep, which could any time be hunted by any creature.

Elena was strong, stronger than me (not in genetic way but in skills), faster than me. But then, she was a human after all. She is weak to the Dark Creatures which are present. And plus, I can't make her life risky just because of me.

It was the day when I had a quick dinner with Elena's mother and her brother. I lied to Osiris that I was going to Trojan's house for a healthy sleep over, as we could grow our love companionship more (not in that way!).

Elena wanted me to meet her mother and even her elder brother as she felt that I was the right guy for her (or something).

I went to her house which was at the end of street. I was greeted by her mother who was really sweet and good. Her brother was a grimacing freak, who just shook tightly my hands, and went off without even saying a sweet 'hi'.

We had dinner. Elena's mother, Claire had made some chicken rolls, some salad, and a huge roaster. It was non-vegetarian which covered the table most.

So there was utter silence in the room. Elena was sitting next to me, and my hand was holding hers under the table.

We ate food in awkwardness, when Claire started the topic, "So Damien, how come you made my daughter flatter on you instantly?"

"It was kind of connection we had. We are much same to each other."

"Oh okay," she replied. "And what do you do...any part time job?"

"Hunting," words slipped out of my mouth as I was stuffing the salad and Elena gave an angry look at me.

Her brother immediately got alarmed, as he ogled at me. Claire was calm as she asked, "Are you a hunter?"

"Uh...uh...yes," I nervously said.

"Isn't it too dangerous that you going with your uncle in the wild where different sorts of animals live?" Claire asked as if she was an FBI agent.

"Not really because..." I started thinking fast; I had to find an excuse when Elena came up with...

"Mom, actually Damien is just in the initial stages. His uncle is teaching him few tricks if he ever gets an encounter with a live animal, you know…" she licked her lips. "Self-defense."

Her elder brother, Dodd spoke, "I hate people who kill animals. I'm going to be a Forest Agent and remove all those scumbags who threaten the wildlife."

Claire patted Dodd's shoulder saying, "Now now, be nice to our guest, Dodd. Everyone have his own choices and maybe Damien has his own."

No! I didn't because my parents stuffed me into this all ram-jam.

After an awkward dinner, Elena asked Claire that can she take me to her room to show some notes. Dodd said that he would also come, but Claire (the cool mother) said that they might need some privacy.

Elena took me through the stairs. I went inside her room. She locked the room, and said, "Whoa, that was bad…"

"Bad, I thought it was the most wonderful dinner I've ever had." I sarcastically said.

Elena made me sit on the bed, and then she came up on me, wrapping her legs around my waist, and taking support of her abdomen on my lap. She kissed my forehead and then my cheeks when she replied, "It could have gone worse, sweetie. You do not want to know what happened when my family met my previous boyfriends before."

I wanted to ask what happened, but then I didn't care much of it. I hugged her, and said, "You are looking beautiful."

She just plainly smiled. "Damien, if you have other things to do, will you go away from me?"

"I think I have to. Responsibilities you know," I seriously got angry—if I had not been have been a Hunter; I would have never been away from Elena.

She kept her head on my shoulder, but she didn't cry. She was brave. She spoke, "I have learnt a lot of about Hunters and stuff—but you know, you never tell me about Lucifer."

She pulled herself back, staring deeply through her starry eyes.

"What do you want to know?" I asked.

"Many things—right now, your life story's main interest is Lucifer."

And I gave a face like: What? Not even me you are interested about.

But well, I started to tell, "I also just learnt in these days when I was in South County. Osiris very often told about few things like Black Skull, portals and other magical stuff. He told me that Lucifer was once a Hunter."

"Whoa, are you serious? But he is your archenemy, am I right?"

"Not only me, but the entire Hunters who are living in this world."

"Cool."

"That's not really cool, Elena." I pouted. "But anyways, Lucifer was a Hunter, he was from a German Legion and his name was Rolf Schneider. His life was the best life as he was the strongest Hunter. He was granted many weapons, gold medals by the Elder Hunters. But well, Lucifer fought against evil and at the same time, his brother was pure evil. He was the Head of Underworld, but was very lazy and all types. So he convinced Rolf to be the lord of Underworld. Rolf with his good heart defeated his brother and made him sleep for eternal life. It is said that he will just wake up one time for the world's domination and then would be finished forever. But anyhow, seeing the power and the control, Rolf was tempted, and he left the Hunters, joined the Dark Creatures. A wizard, Merlin cast a curse on Rolf that he would suffer with hatred, pain and misery. That is why, Rolf turned to Lucifer. He created the Underworld into a more disastrous place and made a portal where every matter or particle can arrive. He was then known as the Creator. His powers were increasing as he kept on defeating much goodwill. But then, a war had taken place many years ago, when he was vanquished, and was thrown down in the tomb which can never be broken until Azazel, his second in command found the code to open the tomb: The Black Skull." I took a deep breath.

"Whoa," Elena said. "I feel as if I'm in Lord of the Rings."

"Uh…can you stop joking?"

"Sorry," she clenched her lips.

We cuddled ourselves on the bed for a while, then had a passionate make out. When I left the house, I felt tired.

Chapter - 14

Nosferatu

It was a weekday when Osiris found out that I was having a serious loving affair. It was really harsh that day, and was one of the worst days of mine.

I didn't know the reason of how he got to know about the affair. But I knew that Athena wasn't the one to tell as she was my best loyal friend.

Osiris was yelling at me saying, "Why Damien?"

"Because I love her, Osiris," I replied to him as strongly as he asked me. "I love her a lot. She makes me feel human."

"But you aren't human, Damien. You try as hard as you can but your destiny is some other."

"I don't care, Osiris! If she makes me feel good, I'll be with her." I murmured, and thought that Dogma was right, I feel humane because I am in love.

"Kiddo, you are risking her life and you must know it. If she is with you, she's in danger."

"I know it," I hate to believe the fact.

It is because I feel really bad. I am risking Elena's life, but what should I do? I can't leave her also. The pain had already stricken inside my blood which pumped hard.

I tried to compensate all the feelings and shrugged my shoulders. The windows were producing the rippling wind which was irrevocably making my eyes steady.

He said, "Damien—she's a human. You know how much advantage the Underworld has now? They can easily take Elena for the bait!"

I didn't listen to him; actually I didn't want to listen to him. I was being stubborn, and I knew that.

"You know what, Osiris?" I stood upright. "I hate this life. I hate what I do. I hate everything of what I really am. I want to be free, I want to become human, and I want to experience humanity, love and joy. I don't want dangers lurking around me and I'm fighting it, I don't want people with disfigured faces hunting, I don't want that I live miserably alone and wait for my death. I don't care about the world also. Why should I? When I already feel myself dead," I added. "And when I felt love and care from someone truly, I thought that I was the luckiest. I know that I'm breaking the hard rules of Hunters and I'm also attracting danger to Elena and me, but you know what? I love her. I want to be with her always, and forever. I don't care how she is or what she is. Even if she's a human, I don't give a damn because she's the One for me and she will always be."

Osiris said, "Then you must await her death. This is your weakness, Damien. Azazel of course wants to find your weakness and destroy it which will make you leave emotionless in this world, and would make you weak."

Osiris was right, he was always right. But it was me, who stayed stubborn and reluctant. Inside, I knew that I'm wrong and he's right, but having an idea of leaving Elena made me just kill myself.

After the hot tempered argument with Osiris, Athena cooled us down. Athena also said that we should otherwise see the brighter side and see that everything will be fine. Osiris and I agreed, but Osiris said that I wasn't wrong either. Osiris spoke that he always wanted the life of a human, but responsibilities and problems and dangers affected his life. Osiris promised that if everything is over, he would of course make no restrictions on me for a human life.

I was back in reality depicted in dreams!

My eyes were still and remorseless. My body fidgety and I grasped for it every millisecond.

I popped my eyes open.

What lay front of me was the most horrific view ever!

Maybe I was in hell. The thought had come in my mind because I was lying down on granite flooring with small pebbles scattered all over. The humidity of the atmosphere was caused by the erupting flames which were in the air.

Oh yes, there was fire in the skies instead of clouds and fog.

I came on my feet to give a good look at the appalling surrounding. I stood up, but immediately realized — that I was standing at the brisk of a cliff.

I looked down the cliff and saw eternal darkness. But not only that, there were groaning and moaning of the deranged, ugly monsters.

I turned back and moved forward. I was in hell, I thought, I am darn sure that I was in hell.

In front of me, I could see a huge cemetery which stretched on the pastures. But the peculiarity lied at the grass which wasn't green, but actually red, as if it had been colored with infinite dead blood.

The cemetery held unmarked and unnamed graves. They were dark, crepuscular and the scariest of all the surrounding, even scarier than the bursting atmospheric flames.

The pastures were cut by a small, rough, path made of stones and gray sand. There were huge boulders at every corner which unevenly stretched at the small terrains.

At the end of intermittent stony path, there was a huge broken cathedral, or so I thought it was a cathedral. Dark huge destructed manor as if someone had smashed the place with a huge hammer. Half of the left side was broken entirely, and even the wind sheets, the topple tower and the wall, cracked and spaced.

I walked spryly towards the manor through the small, narrow path which led me. I knew that Dogma had showed me this dream reality. He always does to me like this. He wants me to let see whatever lay further.

But for the first time, he hadn't accompanied me through the dream. I don't know why. But well, this wasn't a dream. This was reality. It was because the humid atmosphere was felt nuzzling on my skin.

The manor gates were opened already. I came inside, and found myself into abyss of darkness. The small dim red flames gave little dim light to the inside space, and all I could see was demons and vampires jumping with enthusiasm.

They didn't know anything about my approach. They were just jumping in air, as if something good had been foretold to them.

Demons were bear skinned, fleshy looking, and bulged eye creatures. They were all bald headed, and naked. They were wild and dark and scary.

"Where the heck am I?" I asked myself.

I walked up the stairs where the light took me. The stairs were long and elongated which hauled me to the first floor.

One more door was opened with a huge gorge in between.

I came inside. My heart was thumping hard.

The night had crept inside. Only some moaning of demons was heard, even the scorns made by ferocious werewolves!

"Master…" A voice exclaimed.

The lights rounded.

The diffuse flickers showed the marble flooring on a dark spaced place, where a huge throne stood, at the top of some ascending stairs.

Near the throne, lay a huge circulate carpet, where a large, dark figure kneeled down with his head bow down.

"Yes!" A voice said from the throne.

On the large, dragon designated studded chair, sat a man—or a demon to be precise. His eyes were wet green, his skin pure red, two horns on his head like a Mexican buffalo, his hair oiled at the back, and his large tail moving here and there as if trying to find a location to rest.

The throne guy was almost seven feet, with a large suit on himself, covering every inch of his body except hands and feet.

He gave a moan, when the creature near him said, "Master…I will assist you in releasing the one and only Creator, our lord."

The master guy smiled in please, and thumped the arms of his throne badly. Not a nice way of showing his happiness. "Azazel is pleased,"

So he was Azazel. The commander of Underworld army—the second in command of Lucifer!

"I can defeat the one with special powers." The cold voice said. "Or make him join us,"

Azazel frowned in anger. Maybe he didn't like the way he addressed that guy. The one with special powers!

Azazel spoke, "I do not want him around when the Creator will raise, Nosferatu."

"Yes, master." Nosferatu spoke.

"And what would be your malicious plan?" Azazel spoke.

"Kidnap his one and only weakness—his beloved Elena..."

My eyes gaped wide.

What the heck was that?

Elena. I do not think there would be another Elena who would be beloved to someone. All the time, they were talking about me.

I was the boy with special powers. But what are the special powers?

I looked around and saw the clamps of demons dancing. Their wings had sprouted out from their backs, and then they started fluttering in the sky, showing teeth.

Azazel stood up from his throne and waved his hand to make them halt their weird, screeching noises.

"The victory shall be ours. Today is the day we will remember, my fellow creatures. Today is the day, when the Underworld shall be the conqueror of Earth."

He raised his hands up, showing his bare fangs, and grinning devilishly. "Thy End is nigh..."

Chapter - 15

Devious Truth

I woke up.

First of all, I was sweating which wasn't unusual. Second of all, I was shivering, that was unusual. I don't know why, but maybe Dogma wanted me to see this. Dogma wanted that I should know my hidden secretive powers. Dogma wants me to warn that Elena is going to be kidnapped by the ferocious, hidden dark creature—Nosferatu.

But what lay most questionable is…is Azazel planning something really big—like for example—to rise Lucifer from his tomb?

I need to tell this entire thing to Osiris. He can help me. I will not tell him about Dogma, but about the predictions which are coming true.

Only Osiris can guide me ahead. I trust him with my whole heart. Azazel wants me dead just because of my powers. I need to unleash whatever powers I have.

Plus, Osiris can tell me about the Black Skull, which can be our only hope. The Black Skull can raise Lucifer and can also destroy him. But wait—Azazel was talking that they are going to raise Lucifer soon—that means they may have got the Black Skull.

This has to be immediate.

My Earth, my life—can't end like this...and Elena!

I need Osiris but first I have to inform Elena and bring her to the haunted mansion for more safety.

I ran out of my house, with my wiz watch in my hand. I dialed Trojan's number, as I sprinted towards the path which led into the town.

The street lights were dreamy, and the mist was covering the soil tilted roads. The bars and pubs were closed, and the moonlight shimmered its nightmare like a reflection...

"Hello mate?"

"Trojan," I stopped—panting.

"What happened, aye? You look...exhausted?" I was, indeed.

"I need your help..." I grasped. "Elena is in trouble."

"Where should I come?" His voice turned professional. "Is Osiris with you?"

"Right now, I cannot take help from Osiris, bro. It is very rapid. I do not have time much. Plus Osiris won't help Elena."

"Okay...ah...where should I meet you?"

"Come to her backyard and come fast."

I switched off the watch.

CREEK!

I immediately turned back to see where the sound came from. The streets were empty, the fog was surrounded. It was very difficult to see whoever stood in the dry mist.

A shadow moved!

Whatever it was—it was very fast.

My holster was empty. I did not find my Beretta and also my dagger. Now what to do? I must run—that is my only choice.

One more shadow moved…
And so did I.

I reached her backyard, climbed inside her fences, and saw that the lights in her house were gone. Oh skunk! Has Nosferatu come inside and switched off the lights, kidnapped Elena and ran away?

He can't be that fast.

I climbed the branches, approached the canopy as fast as I could. I was sweating. I wasn't good at climbing trees. It really pissed me off. And also Elena hadn't thrown the rope too, so I could pull myself.

I jumped from a broad twig towards her opened window where the wind whistled inside.

I came inside her room, closed the windows, and saw only darkness. The moonlighting could not also enter the room.

I switched on the lights and found…

Elena in her bed!

I was in relief.

I breathed hard and smiled at myself.

She was sleeping hard, with her eyes marooned, her face chalk white, and her lips entirely moist.

I need to wake her up.

I came near her, and twigged her gently. Her eyes opened. She did not scream as a matter of surprise. She just smiled softly.

I looked inside her eyes which looked back at me.

She touched my sweaty sticky cheeks, and spoke timidly, "Why are you here?"

"You need to wake up."

I told her everything. About Nosferatu, about Azazel—

I suggested her to go to my house and stay safe as ever. I also said that Trojan is also coming.

She was scared, she was really scared. She was a fighter, but Nosferatu looked really disturbing and strong. I could not make her life risky.

"What will you do?"

"I will talk to Osiris. We have to prevent the rise of Lucifer."

"So he's rising...?"

"Or he's being raised." I said.

"Let's go...!" I took her arms, and made her come in my back. She grabbed my neck, and I jumped towards the branch.

She did not scream. She was so tensed, that minding me flying in the sky was no worry for her. I jumped down on the ground, damping the grass.

I jumped the fence with her when I found Trojan.

"Are you guys fine?" Trojan asked.

He was with his flute which can change into a two sided double bladed spear.

We nodded our heads.

"Let's go to the haunted mansion." Trojan said.

We were on our way...when it happened.

The mist clouded the road, and it was vastly very difficult to see anything. The street lights flickered ominously. The wind rustled on our faces like a gust—when the uninvited visitor approached.

"You can't leave me alone," a cold voice childishly said. "Especially you, Damien Black!"

A sudden chill went through my body.

The same voice, the same tone...

Nosfertu!!

From the mist, appeared a huge humongous figure. The shadow had crept on his body. His face wasn't seen. It was all mysterious.

But his head was visible, I could just make out that he was bald headed.

"Give me what I want, and you two shall be free." He said.

We turned back to run...

Two demons!

We stayed motionless, looking deeply at the surrounding, where we were held captive in the misty lonely street.

The demons with big green, skinny wing walked towards us. Their smile was wide enough to show their enormous fangs.

Nosferatu stayed on his position. He just laughed. Laughed for some reason — as if he had won the war...his creepy, devilish laughing face wasn't seen till now.

"Well, well, well, I have pity that you three are together. All want to die at one time, eh?" he smiled; he stepped forward — revealing his face.

My heart stopped.

He was different. He was a Vampire. I could make out by his large fangs (bigger than the demons) which touched his chin, his bald round head like a football, and his pale pulpous head. His eyes were yellow. Pure, glimmering yellow which showed that evil stayed inside him all the time.

He was in a long black overcoat which shaded his white shirt. His pants were all shagged up, and it stretched till his ankles. He had long fingernails which he moved vigorously as if he was going to stash me out and his ears, his nose — pointy and dangerous.

Damien Black
The Battle of Lost Ages

The bloodless, chalk white creature's grin was incredibly disturbing. For a while, my mind was like turning over, as if creating madness inside myself. I do not know why.

Trojan unleashed his flute's remarkable power. It transformed into celestial bronze spear, bladed on each side. He stood with me and Elena.

My body felt plain and numbed. My mind was shifting hard. I felt weak.

"Damien...Damien..." The sounds echoed far away from me as if someone was yelling in shrill tone.

All the things in front of me were like a blur. I could see only fragments. It was as if everything was in slow motion. Everyone moving as if they had all the time in this world!

I saw Trojan—he was fighting with his spear, trying his all efforts to defeat the winged demons but he was unsuccessful. He got hand cupped by one hand and his leg, and then they threw him down.

Suddenly we saw Osiris coming with his magic staff. Athena was with him, but this time she was different.

Athena's back had sprouted big white wings through which she glided towards Nosferatu's army.

Osiris compelled Nosferatu ran away whilst Athena burnt out enormous flames from her mouth.

l saw myself back in senses.

My head was having a very serious ache, my body was all drooled out, and my legs were stiff.

I was on my couch, lying with a blanket covered. I heard some murmurings from other room. I tried to hear—just then...Osiris appeared with Trojan and Athena.

"Are you fine, kiddo?" He said. He touched my head and closed his eyes. "He's having fever...high one."

Trojan asked Osiris, "What had happened to him that time? He was blanked."

Athena came towards me. Osiris didn't reply Trojan firstly. Athena, then, just licked me on my forehead, making it all wet with her saliva.

My stiffness and my weakness were all gone now. I felt good, actually I felt great. My entire numbness and weakness had vanished.

"He was weakened by Nosferatu." Osiris replied Trojan now. "Well, maybe Nosferatu wanted him unconscious. He has a power to make people faint."

I touched my head. Somewhat, my head still ached a little. I said, "Now..." I looked around, "Where is Elena?"

Trojan, Osiris and Athena gave nervous, hesitating looks. Trojan said to me, "She is abducted by Nosferatu."

I gave a look of horrification.

"What—how, how it happened...?" I asked, surprised.

Elena was with me. How could she just be kidnapped by Nosferatu?

"We had almost won, Damien. We fought the demons who were trying to hurt you, so you could be safe. But at that time, Nosferatu had taken Elena, and rushed off with his flying serpent." Trojan spoke in a loud voice. "What really puzzles us...why?"

Osiris nodded his head. He was gritting his teeth.

"This is it, Damien." Osiris said, his eyes showed rage and sadness at the same time. "As I had foretold you—they are using Elena as bait."

Athena was sure from Osiris assumption. Trojan nodded his head in agreement.

I sat upright on the couch, with my palms touching my skin. I was thinking deeply and mesmerizingly.

"To get me, right...?"

Osiris shook his head positively. "We are now at the stake of war, Damien. The war has started..." he grasped breath. "And I know the reason."

Osiris had been lost. He was speaking to himself. Muttering with serenity!

"What is that, captain?" Trojan asked, stepping forward.

Osiris pointed at me. "Damien Black!"

"What do you mean?" Trojan asked, shrieking.

Athena remained calm and silent as usual. She was studying everyone's behavior inside the living room, trying to see what was right and what was wrong.

Osiris was showing a regretful expression.

"Damien Black is the main artifact, main achievement for the Underworld. I had expected that this day would come. As I had suspected, Damien is being targeted. And to make Damien come to the trap, they are using a human."

"She has a name, Osiris!" I grunted and stood up from the couch. "Elena…" I narrowed my eyes. She would be in pain and misery, right now with that vampire. "Osiris, why would the Underworld want to destroy me just now…just when I enter South County…?"

"They wanted to find a weak subject, a weak point by which they can hit you." Osiris explained. "They found Elena. That is why Elena is best for them. Human with a heart, soul and fear loathing inside her."

I gave a look at Osiris.

"Why just me—why not Trojan…?"

Athena gave a harsh look at Osiris. Osiris eyes bellowed. Athena nodded. Osiris did the same.

"What is this? Why you always…like…hiding everything from me?" I asked, entirely frustrated. "And now also, you are taking assurance from Athena?"

"Kiddo…you aren't normal." Osiris interrupted me.

I gave a jaw dropping moment. "I know I'm not. I'm not a human." By seeing a not so believable face, I started to have a self doubt experience. "Or am I not?" I asked myself instead of them.

Athena continued. "Do you remember those dreams which you were having lately, Damien? The one where you could see the future or the past…you saw your parents in your dream, and then your father's death by Grimm Reaper. You even saw that Trojan would be found and be not safe in that school dance." She took a deep breath. "Damien those aren't just coincidences or dreams which you were lately having. That's an attribute."

"What do you mean?" Was my first question!

First of all, they didn't know about Dogma. He was the one who showed me most of those realities through dream.

Athena scoffed: "You have power greater than a Hunter, Damien. You are stronger than anyone else."

Trojan gave a look like: *Stronger than me?*

"Your ability is Dream Travel, kiddo. I think you remember I had foretold you about this before. But compulsorily I changed the subject by saying that Dream Travel occurs if there is a medium in between." Osiris creased his forehead. "You can travel to places through your dream. It's basically an out of body experience, where your soul teleports you to different places as a spirit. You also can travel through time but well…it works rarely when your mind really wants to see something. For example, you wanted to learn about more about your father. But instead you emphasized of how his death occurred which made you come in that time." He paused. "Dream Travel works when your mind wants incredibly something like for example, you wanted to know about the missing Hunter. Sometimes your power would be very strong and clear, but sometimes it would be blurred and hazy. We cannot say when your Dream Travel or so called DT works. It is upon you; if you can control your sub conscious as well as conscious."

I was terrified by the thought that I was different. But what really shocked me was my peculiar power. But then — what about Dogma? He said...he had shown me everything. What was all that? If I had the power then how come Dogma was showing me?

Is he a projection in my mind that helps me to use my powers in a more sufficient way? But then — the Underworld, he didn't appear in the Underworld scene, when I had an out of body experience. Where was he then? Did I learn to control my power so well that he wasn't required in my dream now?

I wanted to tell about Dogma so desperately. But instead, I asked something better than that.

"Why didn't you tell me that before? Why now?"

Athena spoke, "We do not have time for all this. Osiris will surely recite you everything you want to know. But first we must talk about Elena."

I nodded my head.

It was the first thing to do. I know that Osiris hid too much from me. But those warm, solid eyes said that he chided for a good reason, as if he didn't want me to know about my powers in this manner.

We all sat in the kitchen where a circular, small wooden table with four stands stood, near to the ebony casketed chairs.

Osiris had his Wiz Comp in which he typed few things.

Trojan gave a hard, sad look. Elena was a good friend of Trojan. Disappearing of her will also make him come in grief.

"Should I use my Dream Travel to know where Elena is?"

"No!" Osiris immediately said, alarmed entirely. "You should not. We all know that the war between Earth and Underworld will start when Damien will die. They want Damien first to be killed as he can be the only savior due to his Dream Travel ability and the intruder between the two worlds. They want to remove that intruding part, and want to enter Earth with a simple way. Or the Underworld wants Damien to be a Dark Creature like Rolf Schneider who was transformed into Lucifer. In that way, they used Elena as bait. So a possible deduction is that Nosferatu will contact us anyhow. We just have to wait for him."

"But we can't!" I protested. "Elena would be in trouble. She would be tortured."

Athena gestured with her head. "No. Nosferatu is a very dangerous, sadistic person. He likes to torture and kill. But he would not harm a fly near Elena because she is the only specific metal which will attract the magnet. In this case, you are the magnet, Damien."

Trojan shrugged his shoulders. "We have to wait then, mate." He kept his hands on my shoulder. "Patience is one of the treacheries in this world."

He was right.

My breath was being wrestled inside me. I just wanted to grab Nosferatu and kill him. I wanted to free Elena now. But—we have to wait. That sucks.

I was standing at the porch, where the low hangings of the green plants were kept. The wind howled immensely, giving chills in my body. My hands were rubbed numerously, trying to keep it warm.

I wanted to stay here, near the shadowy moonlight and the blinking stars. I turned my head down, and gave a low moan.

The hollowness inside me was very irritating. It felt as

if someone had taken out my heart. The feeling of poking and jabbing on my chest was also occurring. It was pain which poked and jabbed.

"What are you thinking, kiddo?" Osiris came inside the porch, from the white windowless door.

"I have questions which aren't answered, Osiris." I replied. "I feel irritated."

"It always happens, kiddo. The feeling stays eternal. Sometimes you know, sometimes you do not." He turned his head to me, after a glance at the sky. "But what you must know is that, some questions should never be answered. It's for the sake of everyone." He continued. "Honestly speaking, I never wanted to tell you that your powers have approached. But well, I had to hide it from you. You are special, Damien. If you can control your Dream Travel, you can defeat and damage the entire Underworld so simply and easily. But it is not easy. You can yourself know, how much your power means in Underworld. Azazel isn't starting war until you are dead or a part of them. He's scared of you more than Lucifer."

Lucifer…Lucifer…Lucifer the Creator…

I don't want him when the Creator will rise, Azazel had said before.

Wait a minute!

"Osiris…" I took a long deep breath. "Azazel isn't planning to create a war between Earth and Underworld— no—he's…" I paused. "He's trying to raise Lucifer and he doesn't want me to come in between."

Osiris poignantly nodded, "then we know his intentions and we know what to do."

I was in my bed, when I woke up.

It was a faint nap which I just had, and which made me feel nauseas tic. I rolled on my bed, trying to think that whatever had happened before was just a plain, suffocating dream.

I turned my head to see an envelope on my cupboard. I picked the crescent crisped envelope, and took out a folded letter.

I unfolded it, and read:

Happy day not so, Damien Black…your love, your precious is with me, huh? If you want to meet her—Come at the nearby under constructed station—she will be free, sire.

The station was actually a train station. It was long and broad, made of wood and iron and steel. The station was scattered with marble granites, and in front of the counter lay railway tracks.

The tracks met a long, closed tunnel where eternal darkness was present.

Osiris, Athena and Trojan had hid themselves, behind the counter, to give a surprise attack to Nosferatu.

I had my weapons beneath my V neck waistcoat. My loose black tie hung on my neck. I was looking professional enough for a fourteen year old boy.

"Welcome, Damien Black." A voice came from back.

I immediately turned back to see Nosferatu standing. His bloodless, cold eyes staring at me intensely, his hunched body wrapped by a silky overcoat with a silver scarf cuffed near his neck.

"So…you have come for your darling, eh?" He snorted happily. "You have come in your own death trap!!"

"Where is Elena?" I came to the point.

"There!"

He pointed back at the railway track. I turned my head, and ran towards the track. I saw Elena, tied to the iron grills with hundred hard ropes. Her mouth was wrapped by a bandanna. She was struggling and trying to escape.

I took my gun out and aimed at Nosferatu, with both my hands clutching his hilt. "Leave her alone. You will die else."

Nosferatu laughed, as he walked towards me. He stopped few paces away, and spoke. "You imagine I would come unarmed like this." He pointed at himself. "Your death awaits, Damien Black. The Underworld shall rise after your death."

From back, huge flapping voices started to come. I looked back, and saw two Vampires sitting on huge winged serpents. The serpents were tall, long creatures, and had large silky skinny tails. Their wings were protruding out from their chest half.

The Vampires were fanning at me with their fangs. Their ears and their pale faces indicated their soulless body form.

Osiris came in the scene, and immediately with his shot gun, started shooting the vampires and even the serpents.

Nosferatu yelled in rage and agony, "You treacherous betrayal!" He ran towards the tracks, when I shot my bullet at his chest, making him collapse on the ground.

Athena was flying too and was battling with the two vampires as Trojan went towards the track to undo the ropes.

I went to Nosferatu who struggled on his feet, but was unable to move. He was shivering and whimpering as he staggered back helplessly. I was deliberately aiming my gun at him, with a cold eye stare.

"Your Creator shall not rise!" I enforced. "I will stop him. I will kill him. You see, after I kill you."

Nosferatu stayed still.

He jumped at me, making me alarmed.

I fell back on the granite flooring, with Nosferatu on my chest. He was trying to sting me with his fangs. I tried to resist, I was pushing him forward. My gun had also fallen down on the ground, few feet away. I was helpless.

A broken rock of the granite had fallen down near my head. If I could only get it, I can be free from this vampire.

His fangs were coming close to me every second, as my hand stretched towards the rock.

I grabbed it and jabbed the rock on Nosferatu's head, making him roll over the floor. He should have been unconscious by that massive hit, but well, he wasn't.

He stood with a dirty, rotten, ugly smile in which his scrawny, wormy teeth were visible. He ran back, towards the track.

He jumped on the grills, and pushed Trojan away. Trojan took his spear, and tried to attack him but was too late.

Nosferatu had immediately enchanted something. A portal got formed in mid air. It was a huge, comfy portal, which could teleport a normal seven feet guy easily.

Nosferatu gripped Elena's arm, and made her stagger inside the portal.

"Fast...this way will not remain always. It will fade." Osiris yelled.

He took his staff and burst two flames out of it, which targeted the Vampires on the flying serpents. Athena's fire ball wounded them, and made them crash beyond the station where they vaporized in air.

Athena climbed down the rail, and said "Let's go!"

Osiris said, "I will hold the portal for you."

The portal was a mixture of many colors as if it had brushed and painted inside it. The weirdest thing was the rotating colors, and showing eternal strangeness.

I nodded my head. Leaving Osiris behind was not a good idea, but there should be a professional who has the capability and endurance to hold a particular portal which separates Earth and the other world.

Chapter - 16

Future of Death

The first thing which came inside my head was actually the worst thing: I thought I was in Underworld.

So why that thought did come?

I was standing on railway tracks with Trojan and Athena on my side. The railway tracks were normal, but the tunnel they met was abnormal. It was broken and scattered to pieces.

I walked up the crushed ground, where I saw damp leaves and scattered vegetation. I saw trees and bushes and flowers, all burnt with enormous humid flames.

The city or wherever I was—darkness had crept like a cobweb. The atmosphere in the black, dark sky was cold and bitter, which poked our skins.

There were creatures or somewhat dragons flying in the sky, with their hooded masks on themselves.

I saw the huge skyscrapers in front of me, little miles away, along the river, where they were broken and crashed. They were all broken, and half separated from each other.

There were many creatures which were visible. Some were monkeys with red eyes, and some were demons with green wings.

Is this Underworld?

Athena sniffed around the railway tracks.

"Damien...this is Earth." Athena answered my question.

Trojan gave a disbelief look. He moved his body around, thinking and seeing, what the heck had happened here?

"Earth...what do you mean Earth?"

"We...we...time traveled, Damien." Athena replied. "This is actually a simulated time. This means that whatever you are seeing will happen in future but this isn't in real time. It's just a stimulus. In another words this isn't real yet it is real, but it is the future."

We walked towards the branches, and the roots of the forest. I saw the internal place of the woods. But it was dark, and creepy. Some weird noises were also coming.

CREEK!

Someone yelled in a screeching voice, and we three immediately crouched.

It was a Dragon.

The Dragon looked at us and then gave one more screeching sound. It was really irritating as if someone was hitting me with a fork in my ear.

I closed my ears, and left the gun on the broken twigged leaves. Just then, another dragon with huge wings, and a mammoth face burst a fire ball at us.

We dodged it but unfortunately I burnt my jeans.

The two dragons gave a wistful look at us, then growled with big pointy teeth of theirs, and then fled away in the dark cloud.

"What has happened to Earth?" Trojan asked Athena.

I was cooling down my burnt jeans. It now had a black spot on it.

"We better must know." Athena nodded her head. She walked inside the vines filled forest, which now lay down at the ground.

She sniffed the floor whilst walking, and we followed her.

I had taken out my dagger which had now turned into a sword, and on my other hand, I had my gun for the protection.

"Someone is here..." Athena narrowed her green emerald eyes. "Something is fallacious."

Suddenly from the muffled bushes, two demons popped out. Their lips were rotten, and their eyes were red with blissful anger. Their horns were tiny and in small inch, their body was in good shape with muscles jutting out. They were six feet above, and with those bare feet, they walked towards us.

Athena emitted angrily, gritting her teeth, and frowning her face. She looked like a mad dog—which she was when ramped.

Someone immediately took my hands, and folded it back tightly, making me leave my gun and sword. The hands lifted me up, and tied me at one of the burnt tree bole.

I realized that it was another demon, and then the same happened with Trojan. But as for Athena, she was tied to the radicals of ground.

From the fallen foliage of trees, Nosferatu appeared with a shuddery smile on his face.

"Welcome to the dark world of ours, my fellow rivals." He squeaked and laughed. "Do you prefer to live here, eh?"

"Mate...we will kill you." Trojan struggled to break the strong knots but was unable to do it.

Nosferatu stretched his rotten, harsh lips into a smile, showing his gritted, wormy teeth. He said, "Trojan Greenwood. What a nice way of meeting, eh? I have heard rumors that you like..." he nuzzled his nose. "Pirates, aye?"

Trojan seemed bewitched.

"There are lots of pirates I know. Even the reanimated corpse of Blackbeard himself."

"Blackbeard?" Trojan mouthed in amazement. "Did you raise him?" He was in utter excitement. He was being under the charm of Nosferatu. .

"Trojan—he's playing with your brain." I hollered.

Nosferatu turned his head angrily. He narrowed his thick, yellow eyes at me. The eventful, scary smile was no more on his face. He was sad and dark and mad at same time. The expressions revealed all of his nature.

He hissed with his long red, sleek tongue coming out, and touching his white pale nose, then touching his skin.

Nosferatu moved towards me, and tried to touch his tongue on my cheeks, but I resisted and moved my head as far as I could.

"Oh, Mister Black...Mister Damien Black!" Nosferatu head rotated in blaze. "You fear death..." He chuckled, and with his pointy hands, he touched my skin. "Not of yourself, but of your beloved."

I did not show through my expressions that I was weak and tired. But honestly, I was brutally scared. My heart was thumping and my body was all—vanished as if. The daunting face of Nosferatu made me timid.

Nosferatu whistled, and two demons popped out with Elena.

She was laid unconscious on the floor, and was looking sweet and cute, but at the same time, tired and troubled.

"She will die for you, Damien Black." Nosferatu showed a pitiful fake face. "You know what?" He asked, but replied immediately. "We never knew where you were, you know. Master Azazel also did not know where you were. But our Creator who telepaths us in our minds informed that you are here." He chuckled. "We were never good at seeking our enemies. But now, look, I never expected that I would catch the Powerful Damien Black." He laughed loudly. "Our Creator awaits your entry inside Underworld or death on Earth. What is the choice you make? But you must..." his eyes intensely captivating me inside his realm. "Know that your beloved's life lies on your decision."

I never thought of becoming evil. I never had that kind of thought. But right now, being provoked by a crazy vampire made me think. What would happen if I use my powers unwisely and change myself to evil? It would be good somehow. I would be stronger, smarter and dangerous. Everyone will fear me and will worship me.

Evil is better, evil is good. And plus, Elena would be saved if I chose the path of evil. She would be my princess, and I would be the prince.

"Damien Black—you are the Prince of Darkness." Nosferatu smiled.

Prince of Darkness...?

My mind shifted immediately.

What did just happen? I was hypnotized by Nosferatu's sleek provocative tone which made me into a greedy boy.

A sheet of arrows struck the two demons on the heart. The other two looked alarmed. Even Nosferatu was alarmed. He did not know what had happened.

From the fallen canopies which were broken, came a huge galloping creature. Yeah, he was galloping. From the upper half he was a human (exceptions like a pointy ear, sharp eyes, and pony tailed hair), but from the lower side, he was a stallion.

Two three small people also appeared from the Centaur's back. They were Dwarves. They were wearing armor, and were having daggers and axes. They were long helms which hid their dwarfish personality. Their face was covered with dirty beards.

"Ahoy!" The Dwarves yelled and threw axes at the demons.

Nosferatu was immediately gathered by the Dwarves and Centaurs.

"ARRGH, leave me alone you smuts, you scoundrels!" Nosferatu grumbled.

The Centaur smiled.

"We have gotten you, vampire." He pulled an arrow and sliced it across Nosferatu's abdomen.

Nosferatu fell down, and staggered back, trying to be away from the Centaur. The horse man just walked, with simplicity and sophistication. He aimed the arrow at Nosferatu's head and...

PHEW!

It slashed across his face, his head, making it burst into pieces.

The Centaurs and Dwarves untied me and Trojan and even Athena. I went towards Elena, and picked her up to see if she's fine.

I checked her pulses, and I realized that Nosferatu was keeping her alive. I was in relief, and I embraced unconscious Elena to my chest.

Then I kept her on the Centaur's back who had told us that his name is Valor and the Dwarf's Head name is Utah.

Valor told us to come with them. They want to tell us and want to discuss few things with me, Athena and Trojan.

We went down the forest, through the steep path which led nowhere. The dark light was reflecting ahead to us as we went deep down the centre of forest.

Finally I saw a red light. A fire was burning.

We went through the clearing and saw many more Centaurs and Dwarves. But not only that, around the circlet of large fire which was ignited by the help of logs, there

These creatures that aren't part of Earth are battling for Earth and as for me who am actually born in Earth; do not even care about Earth.

"Where am I?" A shrill tone came from back.

I turned my head, and saw Elena moving in her bed. She got upright and touched her head. Her eyes small, and her forehead troubled.

She looked around, and then saw Valor, Utah, the Fauns and everyone from the Resistance. She was still and frozen for a moment as if she had seen ghosts.

I came to her.

"It's okay, they are our friends." I assured her.

She still looked horrified.

I patted her cheeks, and put her thoughts towards me. I comforted her and told her everything grumpily before she freaks out and yell.

Finally after the long story of Nosferatu's intention and the time travel (through which I had to tell her in a very low whisper so they couldn't hear), and even the future.

"We are in future. This is Earth." She whispered back, grabbing my hands tightly as if scared.

The nightingale made a jiggling sound which troubled Elena to her worst. She embraced me and kept her head on my shoulder saying, "Please take me home."

I could see the fear in her voice. Even if she was a daughter of a military officer, and well trained (exceptionally), she isn't familiar of these things which I handle.

Chapter - 17

Let's Go!

We set off back to our time.

Elena was in consciousness and she was all set to walk on her legs. We all waved back the Resistance who had persuaded us to stay there and defend against the dark forces, but Athena had negatively said that they are trying to find their home in India (a lie!) and they would of course join forces at the right time.

The farewell had caused no pain and no misery but it caused the worst thing ever in this world:

Guilt!

I felt guilt atmosphere inside me, rounding and making quick gestures, taking and spreading inside my body.

Just due to my own comfort and happiness, I was risking the entire world at stake.

We arrived back at our time and found Osiris standing and holding the portal for us.

He immediately left the portal and it disappeared in mid air.

"So what happened?" Osiris asked us whilst dusting off dirt from his overcoat.

Azazel was scratching his chin. The small circle of light was embroidered on his throne and on himself. The rest seemed dark and gloomy and smelly at the same time.

Near the throne, laid few stairs, from which Azazel climbed down. He walked aguishly around the light path.

"Azazel," someone yelled from the background.

Azazel immediately got alarmed as if he was surprised by the voice which came. "My Lord, is it you?"

Azazel showed anxiety, contempt and fright.

"I am here. Do you hear my voice clearly?"

"Yes, my lord. But how can you communicate with me?"

"My abilities aren't into sleep, Azazel. Some of them are woken up. I can communicate much." The voice spoke. "What is the stage play?"

Azazel was scared to speak. He stammered— "Lord...Nosferatu, my humble servant is dead. He has been murdered, killed by Damien Black. Our backup plan is devised."

The voice did not say in return. It lay quiet, as if thinking something to answer. "Mister Black is a powerful being, indeed." The cold voice struck me. "But we shall not attack him now. I will be the one who will choose his fate. Your only purpose is to raise me from this coffin, from this deceitful tomb."

"But how...how shall I do it?" Azazel face was troubled. "The location of the skull isn't targeted till now."

"Do not locate any more as I know the destination of the skull." The voice said proudly.

Azazel's face bloomed in joy. "Wondrous, wondrous", Azazel says. "Where does the destination lay, my Lord?"

"In the depths of Bermuda Triangle."

"Inside the Triangle, my Lord...?" Azazel spoke, nervously. "B-but Lord...there are Alien Abductions going on?"

"That's just rumors you fool!" The voice prompted angrily. "The Skull's history is unknown. As per my knowledge, the Black Skull was thrown by a wizard many years ago."

"So are you sure that it will rise you?"

"The power of Black Skull is infinite. It can do things which are beyond the possibilities."

Azazel clapped his hands in enthusiasm. "Your work shall be done by Azazel." Azazel bowed to the voice.

"Be quick, I think Mister Black might be watching us." The voice urged.

The voice was omniscient or in another words Lucifer was omniscient. He knew about the Black Skull's location and it was good that I also knew.

Athena woke me up, and we all went in the kitchen, where Peter the Goblin were making breakfast of omelet and bread.

Osiris was sitting on the kitchen chair with Trojan. Maybe giving him more education about Hunters.

They sat frozen when they saw Athena and me. I just said to them, "We need to talk guys."

I told them everything about the dream sequence and how I travelled through the realms of Underworld where I heard Azazel being directed by Lucifer's voice.

I even told about the Black Skull's location...when Osiris asked in a concerned way, "Does this often happen?"

"What do you mean?" He asked me as if I was kidding with him.

"I mean this Dream Travel. Does it happen itself?"

"Not really. Before sleeping I thought of knowing the Underworld's happenings. And then I dream travelled about that. Well, it was because it is really important."

Chapter - 18

The Phoenix Feather

"What can you tell me about a phoenix, Osiris?" I asked. I have heard about the phoenix a little. They were birds with flames bubbling from every side of their body, and they are sacred.

"Sacred bird originates from a fire and dies in a fire…a peculiar mythological being, sighted by Egyptian Archaeologists. You could find them in Egypt as the dawn rises. They flow over the Pyramid of Giza in Cairo. But it is quite difficult to catch them as sunlight is too strong around them. You cannot even see them in the morning and that is why humans lack in the sight of Phoenix. But till dusk, you could possibly watch them, but still they give remarkable light. You would need a fly transport to catch and acquire the feather." Osiris spoke.

"How many feathers do you need?"

"One."

So it was set that Trojan and I would be going to acquire the Phoenix Feather. It would be Trojan's first mission as well as a good training for me too. I was little scared that neither Athena nor Osiris is going with me.

Osiris told us that he would set up an entire cauldron filled with potions until I come back with a red fire flamed feather.

He also told that my Wiz Watch can assist me to contact Osiris and Athena any time, which was a relief as they could help me a bit in an adventure.

Going with an amateur was a bit of crazy idea. I don't mean that Trojan was some stupid guy with a brain like a hamster but I mean that Trojan isn't ready for such a big adventure.

Inside, I felt different as if my adrenaline was pushing through all my arteries and veins were giving me ache in my head and poke in my chest.

I was going to Egypt…Cairo…to catch a freaking fire bird.

I was all armed with my Beretta 92 and my convertible dagger. That was all I needed for my journey. Trojan was also having his flute, and MP5 hung around his back.

Trojan and I were standing out at the porch, where Osiris had said us to halt and wait because our means of transport (in another words flying transport) would be arriving in no time.

Athena was just beside me. She spoke up, "Uh…Damien, you must know that we do not have time. It is a two day time for Azazel to go and fetch the Black Skull. We must bring the ritual items before the two days or the world will—uh—you have seen what will happen, right?"

I nodded weakly.

The fire burning, the darkness spreading in atmosphere, the black dragons rushing around the sky, and the place being deserted—the future would be like that if Lucifer will rise.

So I didn't notice her belt of knives, and a dagger attached to her waist, and even a gun up holstered on her thighs. But when I did, I just knew that she has already planned out that she's going with us.

"No you can't!" I said.

"Yes I can. We are kind of broken up, kid." She narrowed her eyes, and placed sunglasses on her eyes, it was a Harley. "I want to save my world. And serving to save the world is greater than anything in this world."

Osiris immediately came down the porch to see Elena's reluctance. "What are you doing? You can't come. You are a human."

"You are saying as if humans are weak."

"Yes that's true," Athena said.

"You all are wrong." Elena gave a wistful look. "I know that you guys have access to some supernatural things or you have powers which are stronger than a human. But let me tell you. We have humanity and inner strength and emotions which a Hunter, Harry Potter..." she eyed Osiris. "Or a talking dog will never understand."

Everyone was still by her speech except for Trojan who was rubbing Gryphon's back as he was chuckling and smiling.

"And as for combat action, you guys...I am faster and skillful than Damien and Trojan."

Osiris and Athena exchanged glances. I was just glaring at Elena's new façade expression and her new personality— a warrior personality—to be exact.

"Osiris and Athena...she's right." I declared. "What we really lack in our sights is that we underestimate the power of humans which are greater than ours. We always think them as lower people who are just subsided from the saving world part. But we aren't the only ones who have to save the world. The humans also play a big part in it." I said.

Osiris narrowed his eyes. Now it was all upon Osiris. Elena was biting her lips in nervousness, and Athena was calm.

"What did you tell your parents about going away?"

I was gripping Gryphon up by his neck and raided in air with Trojan and Elena. Elena had given her parents an excuse that she was going on a short summer day with her friend, Alicia. It was easy to convince Alicia to tell a lie to Elena's mom about their going out.

Elena also freaked off seeing a griffin. But slowly she compensated her feelings and accepted the fact that an enormous half lion half eagle creature is in front of her.

The ride was awesome as ever. Gryphon glided through the air, cutting between the wisps of wind in between, and breaking all sky barriers.

It was a journey in heaven.

Trojan and Elena and even I were little bit scared of falling down. Gryphon confidently said to us that he will surely catch us up, or if he couldn't then we all are dead. Well, we didn't reply him as it really nauseated me off.

The skies were now shadowing, but the blackness wasn't spreading. The wind was now becoming cold, rippling on our skin and giving shivers to it.

Gryphon wasn't getting tired, and he just sky raced with an intense, deep expression on his face. He increased his speed, and we got a blow by the wind on our faces.

The journey was quicker than I expected. We reached in three hours. Gryphon was really fast, and his wings were strong enough to break the sky winds.

We took rest in woods once on our way. During which we ate food which Trojan had got us for.

Now, as we came on the top of Egypt, and in Cairo, where now darkness had fallen—I saw the huge Pyramids, which looked as if it was touching the sky itself. It was said that pyramids could be seen from outer space also, and now I believe this fact as I see a whole lot big Pyramids beneath my legs.

In the dark, we saw the Phoenix's landing down and crashing behind the pyramid of Giza, by dissolving inside the sand.

"We missed them, mate." Trojan angrily pouted.

"Aw...now what shall we do?" Elena asked.

Gryphon perched down the sands where some light was bestrewed on it. He landed on the glimmering scour, and then started panting. He sat down and relaxed for a bit.

"We got our answer." I said. "We have to stay here for the night."

"On the sand," Elena frowned. "It's so cold out here."

"Hey..." I said. "You volunteered for this adventure."

Elena pouted her face and sat down on the sand, not facing me.

I asked Trojan, "I'm feeling bit of Aladdin...aren't you feeling that?"

"Sure do, mate." Trojan sat down on the grass with me. "I wish we fight a Mummy you know. They are so cool."

I chuckled.

Trojan laid his head down and it was no time that he was snoring lightly. I just gave a wide look at Giza and felt as if it was giving the look back at me. It was difficult to make out its appearance in the black sky, but still the glimpses were enough to give the beauty.

It is almost 400 feet high and it gave goose-bumps to me. Sitting next to the bedrock of the greatest Pyramid made in the history made me feel like King Khufu, the creator of Giza.

I woke up with a light pouncing on my eyes.

It felt really irritating because I felt as if I was asleep only for two hours. Fortunately I had none dreams, as I didn't think about anything before sleeping.

My eyes gave a view of plain desertion. But far away I could see some tourists walking, some coming by the Cadillac's, and some being guided by the guides.

Gryphon had fled away in the sunlight where he was not seen. Trojan, Elena were sightseeing I asked, "Where Gryphon went?"

"The tourists would see him and freak out that is why, he went away." Trojan explained. "By the way, we didn't wake up during the dawn. We all overslept."

Elena was wearing her Harley's glasses. She looked around the sunlight and tried to see if any sightings of the Phoenix flying in sunlight would be present. But the humidity and bioluminescent made her sight to see the invisible.

The tourists with their guides arrived. Some were Chinese and some were Indians, clicking photos, fascinating and jumping around. The guide was an Indian looking man who explained in an Indian way, "So ladies and gentleman…this is Pyramid of Giza, build almost three thousand five hundred years ago. It is said that King Khufu, the mighty Pharaoh, had an advisor, a *vazir* in Indian and Arabian speaking who was the architect of this Pyramid." The guide with a smile said. "Many proves had been altered especially the one during the 1940's when a French hardware dealer found mummified animals which showed no decomposition. It was said that this pyramid, one of Seven Wonders of the World, is built in such a way that it preserves ancient creatures." He chortled. "I wonder King Khufu is also preserved inside somewhere."

The guide turned his head towards us and gave a look of pique at us, and then said with a fake happy voice, "Click some photographs of the Giza, ladies and gentlemen. Then we would proceed inside the pyramid. I must honestly tell you, the inside is plainly beautified."

The tourists nodded their heads in agreement as if understanding the guide normally. They murmured, clicked photos.

The guide came to Trojan, Elena and I, whilst staring with an evil eye. "What are you doing here, you rascals?"

We were perturbed by his expression and his way of talking. He said to me, eyeing in ire. "I know who you are Damien Black. You are plain rascals—you Hunters…I can smell your rat sniff till here." He gritted his teeth. "Leave me alone."

"How do you know we are Hunters?"

The guide gave a choler look, saying. "You played a bad part in my life. You went against us. Your kindred went against us. And now I am living a peaceful life as a normal guide. Do not trouble me."

"What do you mean? I can't understand a thing." I agitated.

"I'm King Khufu, for my sake!" He exclaimed, giving us shock of tremor. "I have been preserved and reformed inside that Pyramid for many years. And now I am free, living like a normal being."

Elena came forward, pushing me back. "Are you seriously King Khufu? The King…oh my gods…I can't speak also."

She shook hands with the guide or Khufu. "I've studied a lot about you. Actually Egyptian History is one of the best History classes I've ever had. And now, meeting a real king, is just plain awesome."

Khufu smiled icily. "Nice to meet you—if you were in my age when I was a King of Egypt, I would have made you wife of mine."

Elena giggled, as Khufu kissed back of her hands.

I pulled Elena back, and told Khufu in a proficient manner. "Listen, we are here to get a Phoenix feather. We will not harm you; whatsoever ugly history you have with the Hunters, it would not affect our companionship. I need your succor."

Khufu profoundly gawped at us for a while. Then nodded his head in agreement—"But it is difficult, young Hunter."

Trojan paced in front of me and said. "What do you mean by difficult, mate??"

"The Phoenix…" he looked up at the candescent skies, and continued. "Is under surveillance of the Guardians, it is a Fraternity which had been set up during the World War during many Egyptian creatures were being killed. These guardians protect the creatures and whoever tries to come in their way, will be utterly eradicated."

So we never expected a society to come in amidst.

Elena scoffed, "Now what?"

I said in valor. "Is there any other way?"

"The Guardians have their meeting every night under the pyramid. They know me very well and at some point revere me a lot. I will distract their minds whilst you catch the Phoenix before dusk."

I nodded.

"Thank you, King Khufu. I wonder why my descendants despised you."

King Khufu said in an abject tone. "I was betrayed by a Hunter long ago. He had assured me that he would help me in the impending battles, but instead he accompanied Underworld."

"What was his name?" Elena perturbed.

He ceased. "Azazel..."

We were all in prostration. "Azazel...the Demon of Darkness...the Second in command of Lucifer!"

"It's well if he calls himself today like that. He was my senior commander, in another infantry of mine. He made me won many side battles against the Underworld. And anyhow, he betrayed me, by telling my frailty to my enemies." He desisted for a while, and then continued. "The Hunters do not despise me, young Hunter...I despise them."

He was in puttered trauma. The bereavement was perceptible by his eyes.

"B-But he was a demon, right?" I queried.

Khufu concurred his head negatively. "He was a normal Hunter. What made you think that he was a demon?"

"Uh..." I equivocated. "Uh...I saw him. And plus he is called Demon of Darkness."

Khufu communed, "Everyone changes..." He was humming now, as if speaking to himself. "In the Underworld...!"

Khufu came back in senses after vigorously shaking his head. He said, "Anyways, we must attain. We do not enunciate and squander our time. I have to affirm the tourists inside the Pyramid. You play off for a while. Shoo—Shoo!" He buggered off to the tourists.

Trojan came forward with an optimistic expression. "So guys, we have stint till dusk. What do you have in mind?"

Trojan, Elena and I had different views upon what to do in entire day. We had time till seven O'clock.

So we all were in Egypt, and each of us was in our dreamland to be exact. We could do thousands of things.

We can go to small Egyptian markets and the Garden City, go around people and ask about the Egyptian tombs which were buried.

We could have done millions of things — but we did the stupidest.

After Khufu went with his tourist group which consists almost twenty to twenty five in number, the front of Giza was now isolated. There were some Cadillacs going to the other Giza Necropolis pyramids.

So we were deserted, and I came up with an idea which I just ensued, "Let's go to Cairo Town. There should be a cab somewhere and then we can explore the city."

"Nah," Elena and Trojan said in unison.

"I'm feeling exhausted." Elena said in a fatigued voice. "I'm so freaking tired!"

Trojan looked up at the sky, and said, "The heat is too much. It can burn us. We need to go and sit under a shadow or so."

I assented by nodding it.

"Just imagine, we are here at our dream place, and now we are here, we do not have anything to do." I replied.

"Let's go inside the Pyramid."

That was a good idea. So we set off towards the tourists led by Khufu. As we walked, on the sand, and towards greatest pyramid in the entire world — we heard a sound!

I looked at Elena and Trojan at back, and found that they were also alarmed by the sound. The sound was like yelling and shouting or so.

"Where's it coming from?"

"No idea!"

"Should we call the police?" Trojan whimpered.

I wanted to call the police. Maybe it could be a grave robbery or so, but we are not sure. "Let's follow the sound." And we did.

We were taking each step carefully and listening to the voice intently. Then finally, after a lot of paces, we arrived at the back of Giza (we were heavily sweating and our clothes were wet; except for Elena, we all were looking sweaty plants)

"That's a boy...right?" I stepped forward, trying to mesmerize my eyes and see if it is the right thing I saw. "That's a boy—he's dissolving inside the sand..."

We ran.

We did not have time as we ran. The boy was shouting, and was slowly dripping inside the heavy sand. His head and his two arms which were struggling showed only visibility.

I immediately took one arm of the boy and Trojan took the other. We tried to pull him, but the force which attracted this guy was massive, and we all fell (even Elena, who was trying to pull him from my side) inside the sand, and dissolved.

So the dissolving part was false as we had hit our bodies down at the basement where perfect granite flooring (yet old) was done and we didn't get killed.

We were in a small passage, which led right and left our sides. The passage was lonely, dark and gloomy, giving a scent of soil, which really made me puke. The place or the underground passage was old, old and creepy, with cobwebs attached at every edge, walls made of marbles but dust covered on it, rocks and pebbles and old marshes which were already rotten, kept around the granite floor.

The place was showing prominent sunlight from somewhere, which gave us visibility of each other.

"Wet magical idiotic sand," The boy mumbled to himself as he dusted off his clothes.

"Where are we, mate?" Trojan asked the new kid.

The new kid was pale dusky. I don't know what kind of color is that. His hair was whipped at the back with enormous oil on it. His body was weak, and his cheek bones were visible. His height was small like Elena and he wore strange multi colored robes, which stretched till his feet.

He looked at us as if seeing a human for the first time and said, "The Underworld's Export Base...I'm mistakenly chosen the wrong path which led me into the wet sand."

We all stared at him as if he knew everything about Underworld.

"What do you mean by Underworld?"

"Oh don't fool me, Hunter. I'm one of the Guardians." The boy said in a serious voice. "I can smell your scent. But I can't smell this girl's scent. You are a human, aren't you?" He asked.

Elena nervously nodded his head.

Hearing a mature, husky voice from a small, innocent guy made us feel that we should never expect anything.

"So..." I broke the long silence. "Why are you here? I thought the meeting was at night."

"I'm not here for a meeting, kid." The boy poked. "I'm here to find my bird, my pet." He gritted his teeth. "The Werewolves had kidnapped her. I can sense Delilah, my bird here. She's here at the base where the Werewolves are trying to suck away her energy so they can be extra powerful."

Trojan neurotically asked, "Pardon me...what about your bird's energy? What does that even mean?"

"Are you blind? Can't you make out that Delilah is a Phoenix?" The boy derided.

Our hearts lightened up.

"Phoenix...can we help you?" Elena asked kindly.

The boy looked at us apprehensively. Then nodded his

head, "What do you want in return? Hunters are always hasty and greedy...so tell me what the deal is?"

"Hey!" Trojan protested, but I made him quiet.

"Okay..." I took a deep breath. "We want a Phoenix feather."

The boy was tremendously jolted by my words, and he collapsed on the hard floor. "Feather...feather...are you serious?"

"Yes, I am. We need it very urgently. We will help you, but getting an opportunity like this could be very useful." I said. "Please, understand this. We need your help."

"Why do you need a Phoenix feather?" He stood up, and dusted off his robes.

I told him everything with some interference of Elena and Trojan. The boy listened intently as if he was in a History class.

Finally...he spoke up, "My name is Ahmad Hussein. And if one feather takes to save the world, then I have no objections."

Well at some point we bragged on. We told him that a Phoenix Feather can save Sun from falling down which is Azazel's real plan. We didn't really lie.

We went through the dark passage, at the right side, as we could hear the moaning and the groaning of a bird coming.

The passage which we strolled upon was visible even in the dark, due to the heavy granite reflection. The place wasn't even that bad, if it could have dusted off little here and there with a good soap.

The lane became steeper now and narrower than before. We had to trudge in a supine way. I even saw some scary rats which jumped from one place to another and whisked off in the tenebrous.

.The narrow path got over and we found ourselves inside a cordon space which was attached by two marble pillars. It was kind of aqueduct form, but in circlet.

We walked over the round place, and saw that under the cordon, was just—darkness. We were standing above an infinite abyss which stretched almost four hundred feet down.

"WHOA!" I got a different feeling when I was at that supine. It felt as if the bridge would swoon down the darkness and we would be lost forever.

Ahmad trailed in front of the bridge which met a narrow path. We entered it, and walked carefully.

We found a glade, where we broke upon and reached a place where some boulders were kept. I realized that the path was connected to a small chamber, which was made out of marbles (but was old and granular). There were precipitous stairs in the middle of chamber, which met a huge circular terra.

On that terra, a huge corral was kept and inside that, there was a hefty bird with inferno all over her body.

The bird was having a large beak, with wings as tall as a human body, reaching outside the grilled cage.

"Delilah…" Ahmad whined.

I kept my hand on his shoulder, and shook my head to stay silent. I pointed at the two Werewolves who were sitting on large boulders just like the ones we are concealed behind.

The Werewolves were puffy and dark. They had long ears, popping out of their heads, hooves which was size of a large baseball. They weren't exactly as I had expected. They weren't those scary looking with grotesque expressions, but instead they were tall and broad.

They were sitting on the rocks like humans, with one leg on other leg, and were playing cards…maybe Flash.

One of the Werewolves said, "Do you have eight of hearts?"

"I can't tell you." The other werewolf spoke. "That's the point of playing flash. You never play card games?"

"I mostly maraud around forests and kill vampires. I don't play these cards." The first werewolf said. "ARGH…I can't wait more. When would master Azazel come?"

"Uh…in just few hours."

The first werewolf grunted and heaved the cards down at ground. "I do not want to play. Let's watch the bird."

The werewolf came up to the cage and enthralled in enthusiasm. "She's so beautiful."

Delilah wailed in anger.

The second werewolf said, "Bubba…move away from the phoenix. She can burn you by a touch. Her flame power is enormous."

Bob backed off.

"How do they talk in fluent English?" Elena asked, baffled.

"They adapt themselves according to their surroundings. They maybe from America as they are good at English or maybe from Britain, and that is the reason they can speak good English." Ahmad explained.

Whatever Ahmad had explained wasn't known by me. I was pretty much impressed by Ahmad.

Trojan armed his hands with his flute spear. He spoke, "Let's go mate. Let's bash those dog heads."

Ahmad twitched, and flustered in anger. "No! These Werewolves are dangerous. They can massacre us in seconds."

I was mesmerizing in my minds. Trying to find a perfect, yet disturbing solution!

"Distraction," I popped with an idea. "We need a distraction, guys."

Ahmad nodded his head with a slight smile. For the first time, I had seen a smile on that wrath looking face.

I took a rock in my hand and with an assured nod; I threw it on the left hand side. The werewolves immediately got alarmed, and bared their enormous bloodshed looking fangs.

We promptly ran towards the cage as the Werewolves jumped at the rock. They realized that it was just a rock, and looked back.

Their white pupils watched, as their saliva dripped from their dog like faces. With heavy muscles and broad shoulders, they bolted towards us.

I took my Beretta. I knew that my Beretta had silver bullets, fragility for a werewolf. But I was scared. My hands were shivering, and my heart was clouting immensely.

I was scared that if I mistakenly aimed somewhere else, the werewolves would whack us and eat us alive.

Their petrifying faces were gruesome and repulsive. I had to shoot the silver bullet. It was our only chance of winning over them.

BAM!

The bullet opalescent at one werewolf at the chest, as he collapsed backwards!

Bubba was dead—or maybe the other wolf. The two looked the same for me.

Ahmad, Trojan and Elena were trying to open the cage, as the second werewolf leapt towards us.

Trojan stabbed his spear in the werewolf's chest. The blade went through his hairy chest, while he croaked and moaned in pain and misery. Trojan with the help of spear threw the werewolf body at the boulders where the two played cards.

We were saved.

Damien Black
The Battle of Lost Ages

Delilah was carping, lamenting and deploring in spasm.

Ahmad said, "The cage is too strong. It cannot be broken."

The tribulation in Ahmad's eye was too much. I had to do something.

There was a small tunnel like entrance, at the top of Delilah's cage, joined with the guttery ceiling. The tunnel met at a hole in the desert.

I heard cries and whines.

I looked up and saw a dragon coming through the tunnel. But not only that, there was a man sitting on that dragon.

When would Master Azazel come?

Bubba had said that.

"Run!"

I took Ahmad by his shoulders, and with Trojan and Elena, I whipped past the cage as the dragon landed near Delilah.

On the dragon, I could see a man with a shadow covering half his face. But his venomous tusk was foreseen, and his red skin too. He took off his hood, and grinned at me devilishly. He was in his same suit like appearance with his horns glinting more than before.

"So...we meet at last, Damien Black." Azazel said in a husky, deep voice.

The dragon tusked and burked. His long tail with a spade, and twigs attached gave baleful torment. His eyes red like Azazel. His body black and dark likes the moonlit sky. He wasn't large, but he wasn't small too.

"I see you have killed my servants with your friends." Azazel looked at the two werewolves, laid unconscious.

Seeing Azazel for the first time in reality made me feel a little—embarrass. I don't know why but I felt it.

"Why do you need Delilah?" I said.

Azazel smelled deeply redolence which is snipping in the air. He gave a shudder, and then ranched. "What do you desire to know?"

I narrowed my eyes. What the heck did he mean?

Ahmad suppressed. "He's confusing you. Be careful."

I nodded my head. I was trying to be smart.

"I desire to know about the usage of phoenix." I said. "What is it, Azazel?"

"And what made you think I would tell you?" He said.

He was right. He wasn't some quirky, idiotic villain who will appraise all his evil plans to the heroes, you know.

Azazel's dragon grabbed the cage with his unguis. Then Azazel said, "The world will end. Lucifer will take his revenge on Earth and we shall be free from that flaming world."

I aimed my gun at Azazel. "I'll kill you, you bloody snout."

He voided his head. "No, no, no...my dear—you can't kill me. That is not your destiny."

I wanted to press the trigger but—I couldn't. I was still and frozen, as if someone had said something very indirectly to me, and somehow I understood it.

"Something is obviating in Damien." Ahmad remarked. "He isn't a normal Hunter." He smelled the air. "I can sense a different sort of blood in him."

Azazel beamed.

He sloshed up the tunnel with his dragon and the cage. I was barely still.

Elena slapped me hard.

"Ouch!"

Lucky me, I was back at my senses.

Trojan asked Ahmad, "What was wrong?"

"I-I d-don't know." Ahmad sniveled. "For the first time, I can feel strangeness. But at some point I have no clue about it."

Elena, Trojan, Ahmad and I— all were quizzed. But then I spoke up, breaking the silence, "We do not have time. Can you call Gryphon your best friend?" I turned over to Trojan.

"Ahoy!" He nodded.

He stood up under the long tunnel, and whistled so obstreperously that it shook the entire chamber.

For a while nothing happened. Then suddenly the griffin strode the tunnel and smiled mischievously, "Mate, I told you that I can hear your whistle many miles away also."

Trojan smiled.

I rushed towards Gryphon and asked: "How fast can you fly?"

"Faster than a dragon, mate." He had become Trojan's pirate friend.

"Let's go then!"

"Ahoy, captain!" He smiled.

"I will come, guys. Meet me at the surface and get Khufu. We would be in need of the other Guardians for the assistance."

Elena came towards me, and spoke softly. "Be careful. I love you."

"I thought we had a break up."

"Idiot," she said under her breath and kissed my lips tightly. "Run away my hero."

I grinned. I didn't care who I was or whatever Azazel meant by saying me about the destiny. I didn't know why Nosferatu also had said that I was Prince of Darkness. But one thing I knew very well. I was Damien Black, the Slayer.

"Shall we go, captain?" Gryphon asked.

"Ahoy!" I clamored.

Gryphon and I were up the sky, and into the enormous sunshine which reflected on our bodies. Scintillate of light was really irritating as we rushed towards the shallow side where the clouds had been formed.

The tourists and the Egyptian people were nowhere in the plain desert.

And even Azazel with his large dragon had been just disappeared. Gryphon said, "I cannot see anyone, master."

"Me too."

It was true. The skies and the gleam of sun were mixed together and were producing radiations around.

From the upper welkin, the dragon of Azazel raced down, extricating the heavy sturdy cloud.

He was having a spear, a bow in his hand through which he pointed his arrows. I took my Beretta and my dagger which turned into a complete astral bronze sword.

Gryphon flew under the dragon, so it was difficult for Azazel to shoot his arrows. But Azazel wasn't quite stupid. He immediately turned over his dragon, by somersaulting it, whilst the cage moved vigorously and the Phoenix cried in bitterness.

I just had to shoot the claw which holds the cage, and the phoenix would be free from it. But the heavy gust and the winding haze made me difficult to handle the gun.

My body was moving strenuously as Gryphon was trying his best to come in level with Azazel's dragon.

Azazel shot his arrow (and I realized that it was dipped inside a poisonous potion), but Gryphon rolled his body in the air, preventing the attack.

I shot several bullets, at my best.

Some of them hit the dragon's wing (did not affect him at all) and some of them were disintegrating inside thin mid air.

Azazel screamed, "Damien Black—you shall never win. You killed my apprentice, Nosferatu, and now you shall repay."

I didn't want to tell him that I wasn't the one who killed his apprentice. It was actually a centaur from a simulated time whose name was Valor.

"Didn't your creator…" I yowled, "said that I'm the least of your worries right now?"

And it hit him.

He was blank and serine. His eyes were showing tranquility. His body was inert by bewilderment.

I got my chance.

His dragon was bellowing and was coming to our level of flight because Azazel was surprised and wasn't controlling the dragon properly.

I immediately aimed at the claw…

BOOM!

It created an explosion from the barrel which hit the claws of the dragon making the cage fall down.

The toppling cage was taken by several Pegasus. On those Pegasus, men with bushy beards, and bald heads picked the cage up, and destroyed it with their staffs. So the Guardians had arrived there to help.

The Phoenix broke apart in the air, and it rose through the sunlight, joining the large sun at last.

Azazel was nowhere in the sky.

Chapter - 19

The Secret of My Father

"Thank you Damien Black."

The man would be in his forties. He had a trimmed stubble beard on his chin part. His eyes were pure water blue and his head was covered with a small, round hat. He was wearing a large robe, multi colored same like Ahmad. His voice was very cool and sophisticated, giving a sense of relief, happiness.

"Welcome," I smiled.

The man slapped Ahmad's head, and spoke, "Fool, you could have foretold us. Why did you risk your life?"

"Father, I'm sorry." Ahmad groaned while touching his head. "I was worried. I wanted to know where the werewolves had taken Delilah."

The man gave irascible face at Ahmad, but then changed his expressions. "Anyways, Damien Black, you have deeply expedited us. If anything happens and you need help, you can reach us through Gryphon. He will inform me and the rest of Guardians."

I nodded my head humbly.

"And one more thing…" He clapped his hands.

Two Guardians with heavy beards and dark bloodshot eyes walked towards the man with a small casket in their hands.

The man presented the casket towards me and I caught a hold of it. I looked inside the casket with Trojan and Elena on my side. We all looked at it as it shined and glimmered deeply.

"The Phoenix Feather," I muttered.

It was a long, silky feather, looking as if brittle and frangible. It was deep red, as if blood had splattered on it, and was giving a little black touch to it.

We thanked them, and after the farewell to the Guardians, we met Khufu who had played a big part in this battle with Azazel.

"Thank you for isolating the pyramids and the desert."

Well, no one saw me fighting a dragon and sitting on a two mixed animal kindred. With help of Khufu, the tourists and many of other people had been evacuated as Khufu had told that there was an earthquake, which creates slight cracks on the ground.

And from far away, due to intense sunlight, no one could see that two different people were fighting in the sky.

We thanked Khufu, and Elena took some photographs of him, keeping for her album of Historical People She Met Book by Elena Sanchez.

We set off for the journey back. But the journey wasn't over. The Skull wasn't found, I guess because Azazel was up to something to do with the Phoenix. One of the Werewolves was foretelling that Azazel was absorbing the source of energy from a phoenix as this bird consists of very high light energy.

I do not know for what reasons.

But what I do know is that, we have a journey to find the Faerie's venom.

On our way to South County, Trojan asked: "Hey what did Ahmad mean by saying *'He isn't a normal Hunter, I can sense a different sort of blood in him'*?"

"Only one man can answer that question." I mumbled but it was overhead by Trojan who held the casket and even Elena.

All the way back home, I was thinking about Dogma. His faceless features, his bright eyes, his heavy cupid face, his smooth hair, his tall body, his large wings. He was an angel, or much looked like one.

Dogma wasn't a Helper now. Maybe I know the reason. Maybe he was just a helper until I didn't realize my Dream Travel powers fully. And now when I'm sure about the powers, he will be of no help.

But then why didn't he tell me before about my powers if he knew about it? And why he isn't coming in my dreams anymore?

It was all complex. First he wanted to help me, and then he doesn't want to tell me my powers. But maybe Dogma itself didn't have any idea about my power…uh…but then he told me that he showed me my past, of my birth and my father's death, actually it was my power which showed me that.

I have no idea about Dogma, and the more I think about it, the more I get intricate about all this Dream Travel.

I had to make things clear:

I have a power, I have a helper, I do not know anything about the power's use by Dogma himself, and I have no idea that Dogma knew about my powers.

So this is like a jigsaw puzzle.

Plus one more puzzle is formed. I have a different blood, different from a normal Hunter. What the heck does that mean?

Azazel is after Phoenix to absorb the source of heat energy, and also none of us know don't know that the Skull is located by the Underworld creatures or not.

We approached the haunted mansion where Athena was waiting for us. Gryphon went for a drink in the river which was near my house.

We set off inwards, where Osiris and Athena listened to our story intently. We told them everything including Ahmad's saying about me. We also told them about the source of energy which Azazel was trying to absorb by the Phoenix. We also gave them the Phoenix Feather which he kept inside his little spelled cabinet.

Osiris and Athena gave fidgety gaze at each other.

I understood what that look was.

"Oh no...not again...now what you have hided?" I was getting used to this secrets latent inside them.

"First we should confer about the Phoenix Absorption of Sun Energy." Athena affirmed.

Now I have to be accommodating until they reveal my indigenous secret.

"So what is it?" Elena asked keenly. "Why did Azazel need that kind of thing?"

Osiris kept his one leg on another, and moved his hands rhythmically. "Phoenix has the calefaction energy, in words heat energy. The heat energy radiates almost half of the Sun's energy. It is one of the most powerful energies in the entire universe to be said. It can be used for several purposes. It can lighten electricity of an entire Earth; it can build extraordinary potential inside a particular person or a creature. So I conjecture..." He desisted. "That Lucifer would be weak and tired living in a tomb for millions of years. His omnipotence powers would be vulnerable and trounced. By dissipating the heat energy of a Phoenix would cause Lucifer to generate his old, ancient, evil powers." He sighed. "But the good thing is that, we have prevented it and he would not be able to increase his susceptible powers."

So this was really dangerous. I was the hero in saving the world from virtual omnipotence of an evil—yuppie, I had won.

I was being childish, sorry.

"Would he be up to something else?" Trojan asked.

Osiris stood up, not refuting Trojan's question. He went to a small globe stand, which was the very new thing I had seen in the living room. He took the globe, leaving the stand at that place, and touched one segment of the sphere (which was the sea, maybe).

A hologram formed (like Star Wars movies and Star Trek, you know what I mean right?), evincing an entire army with red heads, big scars, tall bodies, heavy muscular arms, and fleshy skin, walking and jumping up the board of a ship.

On the deck, Azazel stood with a spyglass in his hand (it was weird as the hologram was barely perceptible), and looked elsewhere. His small dragon laid behind him, moaning and groaning as if trying to utter a word to Azazel.

Azazel replied, "We shall find that skull and release our creator, Flagon—we are far but we will come near. We have to be easy on our defenses. The Triangle plays tricks which no one can ever conceptualize."

Flagon shrieked loudly, and Azazel replied, "I think so the Hunters are up to something. But we shall not waste our time in hunting the Hunters. We must raise our Creator and he will deal with these minor problems."

Flagon shook his head, nodding in agreement and seated his head on the wooden deck, sheepishly.

The hologram switched off automatically, and Osiris kept the globe back at the holder. He spoke, "This is Trajectory Transmitter which enables us to see the ongoing of our enemies in a very limited time. But it does not always work as it suppose to work." He looked at Trojan. "I think you got your answer."

Trojan nervously nodded.

I asked, "What about the blood, Osiris? What did Ahmad want to say but couldn't?"

Athena answered the question. "Ah, Damien we hide a very fragment of your life and past. You never asked us one thing: How did you acquire those peculiar powers which a normal Hunter does not have?"

She was right. I never asked. What a fool I am?

"How did I?" I rumbled.

"You remember about your father's death which was caused by Grimm Reaper himself, eh?" Athena asked and I nodded. "You saw those moments, that pain and that death and you heard those words because of the Dream Travel. In real, you asked us that Death kills only those who cheat death...am I right? And we answered that Death was working with Azazel—we lied to you!"

Another lie!

"I am sorry; we did not want to disclose everything at once." Athena lowered his eyes. "You saw the birth of yours in St. Cross Hospital, remember? Oh yes you do. You saw your parents. But you didn't see something more wicked. You were lost in your parent's memory that you didn't notice the peculiarity in his appearance."

And then it hit me!

The pale red skin, the pointy ears, the jet black hair with oiled at front, and a tall, muscular body—my father's real appearance came in front of me like a jaguar!

"Your father was a demon, and he cheated death several times."

I could have fainted down or I could have jumped down in an ocean, and drown myself to death.

"You have special powers which you, I or Osiris does not know about just because you are part demon, part Hunter."

Trojan thumped my shoulders, "Mate that is why Nosferatu wanted you to come in Lucifer's army and even Azazel meant by saying that this is not your destiny. Maybe he meant that your destiny lies in Lucifer's army. Mate, don't you understand?" Trojan was finding something optimistic about it. "They will not kill you, Damien. They *want* you, because you are powerful than ANY OTHER HUNTER OR DEMON."

I looked at Osiris and he had nodded his head gently indicating that Trojan was right on his stupid talk.

"But what does a demon mean? If demons exist and then angels also," Elena asked, stepping forward. "Where are angels?"

"There are no angels and there are no demons. What we call a demon is actually a new hybrid created by Lucifer himself which he has officially named 'Demon' which signifies that it is dark evil." Osiris elucidates.

I was beginning to realize that my father was a demon and my mother was a Hunter. Which means that I have demon blood inside me, which means that I am a half demon—which means that I'm already in Lucifer's army of demons? I was freaking out!

I am scared. I looked at my hands. Those small, bony hands, were giving me a demonic look and saying, "You are a demon, Damien Black. You are not any normal Hunter."

I was self seeing these things. My insanity was reaching to the peak. My heart beat was pounding heavily and my pulses were throbbing fast.

Athena gave a look of "I knew this would have happened." And she turned her dog head towards the window, where she glared outside.

Elena, by seeing me in this condition of astonishment, comforted me by hugging my shoulders, and wrapping her arms around me. She didn't care that I was a hunter or a demon, she just didn't care. So why should I?

Oh my gods!

I'm losing my marbles!

Osiris clapped his hands, "So, Damien—we do not have quality time to spend. We have to collect on more items for the ritual. The cauldron is filled with the material which we needed, and only Faerie venom is required."

I didn't question him.

Trojan asked, "A Faerie, captain?" He was puzzled. "How come a Faerie has venom inside her, aye?"

Osiris went into his study room (not replying Trojan's question which made Trojan irritate and embarrass a little), and came back with a large hardcover book in his hand.

He flipped the crisp yellow pages of the book, and came up on a page, where we saw the designated diagrams of different sorts of Faeries which are present in this world.

He read a small paragraph which was underneath the illustration of a Faerie with big ears and big hair.

"There are different kindred of Faeries. Every kindred has an exception to each other. For example the Faeries known as Topples are the loving and healing Faeries who like peace and harmony. They have a way to sting their tail at a particular creature or person and help him to cure any disease, or wound. But Topples are the mildest Faeries. The worst and the evil Faeries which are from the place called

Underworld are the Bollix, who live peacefully but do not want anyone to disturb their peace. The Bollix has a special sting in them, venom or a bane which can poison anyone in a millisecond." Osiris gravely said.

We all stared at him for a while—shocked.

"Doesn't this journey need an adult on the way?" Trojan asked, weakly.

Elena also nodded. She was trying to be brave, but her hands were shivering vigorously.

"We have an adult." Athena declared.

Our faces lightened or at least Trojan and Elena's.

So we almost guessed that maybe Athena or Osiris would be coming with us, but all our guesses and assumptions crashed down when Athena called out:

"Tootsie,"

Elena and Trojan gave slight, unison looks at me, and I shook my head, replying "Never heard of this name, guys."

The creaking footsteps approached the stairs, and from the crepuscular shadow, approached a figure, revealing his demeanor to us.

"Hello, buggers—how are you?" It was a British accent which came out of the mouth and I was pretty sure what stood in front of us, wasn't a British at all.

Chapter - 20

A Fairie's Venom

She was a female that much I could make out. But she wasn't a human female, she was a —a —Faerie, I guess. I've learnt few things about Faeries, and all those characteristics were in Tootsie.

Her body was short, shorter than any of us in the group. She was almost four feet, like a small kid in a fifth grade, but her face and the voice was mature for her height. She had glistening chestnut brown hair, which was tied in a knot by small leaflets. Her skin was green, plain pale green with small dark circles under her brown eyes.

"So, my name is Tootsie, kiddoes." She shook hands with each of us. "You are a human, oi?" She asked Elena.

Elena nodded. Now she was getting pestered by everyone who downed her by saying that she is a human.

"So are you ready, you little buggers?" She jumped in the air.

"Pretty much," I replied.

She nodded strongly, and said. "Let's go!"

We were in the air with Gryphon and were heading

towards the seas. I did not know where we were going as it was difficult to make out.

Tootsie was controlling Gryphon better than me or Trojan. Elena sat behind me, muffling her hands around my waist, with her head on my shoulder and a shroud expression on her face. Trojan was at the back, getting bored.

"Where are we going?" I asked Tootsie.

It was funny that a small creature, a small Faerie riding a big Griffin.

"Have you heard about Robin Hood, sire?" She asked me, and I would have said, "Duh, who has not?" but I just replied sophistically:

"Yeah, a lot."

"Have you heard where he lived?"

"S-S..."

"Sherwood!" Trojan spoke from the back.

"Exactly, and where is this Sherwood, sires?" Tootsie asked.

"Nottinghamshire," Elena spoke.

"Which is in?"

"England!" I replied immediately, not giving a chance to Elena or Trojan. "We are going to England?" Now I understood.

"Yup—and in that Sherwood Forest, in Nottinghamshire." She grumped. "Oi."

After several hours (It felt a longer ride than the one from Egypt though geographically it wasn't), we landed in a dandles of forest, where canopies and foliage was covering the entire forest.

We came down on the ground, and stood on the broken leaves, and the scattered pebbles. There was only vegetation and greenery everywhere. But it felt fresh and good, and not like the one we dealt in the simulated time where Nosferatu took us.

The light was advancing in the clearings of forest, and giving luminosity palpably.

The vines, and the twigs, the branches were entangled, and even the different sorts of trees were in conjunction.

Trojan said to me, "Spooky, aye?"

"You mean beauteous, eh?" I chuckled.

Tootsie patted Gryphon's head. With a sweet farewell, Gryphon went off in the sky as his job had been done and he would be summoned when it is necessary.

Tootsie took out a small rectangular device, on which an antenna was attached. The device showed some speculations and gave croaking sounds. Tootsie said, "We must move ahead, kiddoes."

Trojan and Elena were with me, side by side. Trojan had taken out his spear, whilst Elena had taken out her gun. I took out my dagger, but did not change it into a sword.

"What are we dealing with?" Elena asked, keeping a stern look at the forest and on the soggy, sodden leaves.

"Bollix leader."

"What is her name?" Trojan asked, timidly.

"Malice," Tootsie said. "She's evil, just you should know."

"I can make out by the name." I said in decrepit.

We walked inside the shrubs which were stuffed together. We came into a small place where vines, fruits, flowers, plants were separated by a small stony path.

"This place is mostly used as camping, festivals and other things. You may be familiar about it, right?" Tootsie asked.

We shook our heads negatively.

"Okay," she said dully. "Anyways, so this makes the Bollix Queen, Malice really raged as her peace is destroyed. As a creature from the Lowlands, she is strictly been captivated inside a small cave where once Robin Hood lived." She explicated.

"Okay two questions," Elena asked. "What do you mean by Lowlands, and also, why did you say that 'where once Robin Hood lived' as if he was real?"

Tootsie stopped her tracking from her device, and gave a stern look at Elena. She looked at me and Trojan for some answering, but honestly speaking, we ourselves didn't know about this.

She sighed in frustration. "Buggering Bogart, the Lowlands is a place where Faeries exist. It is said that all the kindred and specimens of Faeries had been evolved in Lowlands. It is said to be under the Earth, deep down, where no digger or a human has gone."

"Aye," Trojan muttered in excitement.

"And my question?" Elena asked.

Tootsie suspired and said, "I meant that Robin Hood is real."

My face wasn't flummoxed like Elena and Trojan's bemusement faces. I knew about Robin Hood, about King Arthur and about the One.

"What?" Trojan and Elena said simultaneously.

Tootsie gave a grave look, and I understood what she meant. She turned her body, and she began her trailing without answering Trojan and Elena's question.

I began to say, "Robin Hood is real. Whatever folklores you have heard about him it is loosely true. It is because, he was that guy 'Steal from the rich and give to the poor' but he was a Hunter as well. Robin Hood's history is little blurred and no one knows that he's *actually* true or not as it remains a question. No one has seen him till now, but many Hunters at his time believed in him."

"What more?"

"The One...King Arthur were one of the Hunters as well."

Elena was tremendously shocked.

"The One...?"

"The One started the first Hunter Legion by giving them extra powers than humans. He gave it because he wanted a secret army finish the evil on Earth. After his death, the Hunters mourned that their leader had been dead. But his supernatural powers remained in those Hunters and from that time, Hunters were slowly generating. Even King Arthur was a Hunter, and a major Hunter who led a war against Lucifer's predecessor, Soul. We needed magical weapons; we go to Nicholas Flamel, the alchemist who only doesn't create the elixir of life as it was just a small creation of his, he also creates different sorts of magical swords, guns, daggers, sabers and he's still alive."

Tootsie added, "John Dee, the famous navigator, magician, mathematician, astrologer etc was a captain during the war with Lucifer."

The two were fascinated by this talk. I hadn't told them the entire story and all which Osiris revealed to me in entirely just before we left for this expedition, since he decided not to conceal anything from me about the Hunters, because if I did, they will forget that we are here to kill Malice, the Bollix leader.

"Who is Soul?" Trojan asked.

Tootsie replied, "We don't believe in him because according to the historians, Soul never existed. But the sources from corner of world have disclosed that Soul was pure evil and his only motive was to *oorwin die heelal*."

"What is that?" Trojan asked.

"No one knows and no one wants to know. It is because no one believes in Soul and we want to keep it that way."

Trojan and Elena hesitatingly nodded.

We finally came at the end of stony path. We skipped the bushes, and I enthralled my Beretta out of my holster.

Elena also took her gun out, and Trojan took out his spear.

We came in a small part, where a big cave was standing in front of us. It was a gloomy looking cave which met a big stone wall. Near the cave there was a small river, a narrow one, hitting the small terrestrial rock.

"She's in there, oi!" Tootsie said. "She can play tricks, kiddoes. Be careful!"

Tootsie took her small knife which looked like a sword in her hands. She stepped forward, and walked bravely when someone hissed.

"Faeries—I smell Faeries."

Tootsie immediately directed us to shut our mouths.

Tootsie spoke, "Yes, it's a Faerie!"

"Oh my beloved Tootsie," the voice charmingly said. "How nice of you to come here."

I couldn't see the hissing person, but the way she was saying, it really gave me chills and goose-bumps on my arms.

The figure came out of the cave and it was the first time we saw Malice appear.

She was tall, taller than Tootsie. She wasn't looking like a Faerie at all; instead she was having a personality of a princess. She was incredibly young (looking in her twenties) and was beautiful with marvelous façade design. She had blond, round hair which fell till her back, her blue eyes sparkling with grandiose transcendent.

But what I didn't notice was the long wispy tail which strand from one place to another.

"Well, well, well..." Malice grinned, showing her perfect, white teeth. "You have brought Hunters..." she looked at Trojan and Damien with a sensual smile, and I

pretty much think that she likes me. "And a human, also," Elena groaned in uneasiness.

Tootsie said, "We need your help, Malice."

"Oh, really…?" Malice gave a shocking look but her expressions seemed fake but perfect.

"Yes."

"And where the sun had risen today, eh? My own blood sister wants my help." Malice spoke.

We were in utter shock!

Tootsie is Malice's sister. Tootsie gave a jittery look. But she stayed still and brave. She told everything about the urge of need for the venom of a Faerie. Malice listened intently but for most of time, she was admiring me and winking at me. My heartfelt a putter joy, whilst Elena groaned and gave evil faces.

"Why can't you give your venom, eh?" Malice asked, stretching her brows up.

"You have a sting?" Elena was shocked.

Tootsie hesitated.

"Oh yes…she had once, a sting." Malice provoked. "She was the best girl in our family." Malice rounded around Tootsie with an evil expression on her face. "And I was the black sheep. She lost her sting due to her lover…"

Tootsie shivered in her revelation.

"She killed a friend of ours when he tried to stop the lover with her sting and lost all her venom at once." Malice waspishly said. "And you know what?" She looked at us.

Those beautiful eyes watching Elena, me and Trojan!

"That friend was my lover and Tootsie's lover was a human." She exasperatedly looked at Elena, her eyes turning pale white. "And my lover was a Hunter!"

The next thing—I don't remember anything.

I woke up on a small harsh floor, which was gritted with

rocks and pebbles. The soil was soft but hard also. The sunlight poured at a minimum rate. It was quite after sometime that I realized, I was inside a cave.

The small cave which was of Robin Hood once wasn't as small as I had expected. It was actually an entire cubicle with rocks and terra's kept.

On a big rock which was shaped like a throne, was being used by Malice for sitting.

In front of me was Trojan, half injured. I looked at myself and found a wound at my knee. It was unbelievable that blood clot was on my denim jeans.

I didn't saw Elena and Tootsie anywhere. They were absent from this place.

"Oh my poor Hunters," Malice spoke up, while coming down her throne, and greeting us with seductive smiles. "The two of the girls have left you here in this creepy dungeon."

I couldn't believe it. I couldn't believe Elena.

Trojan was giving the same eluding face at me like I gave. Malice spoke in saccharine tone, "My Hunters, I want a husband for myself, a lover who can tender me and love me." She twinkled lecherously. "Who wants to be my lover and stay with me?"

"I want to be!" Trojan and I said immediately at the same time.

We looked at each other in anger and betrayal. Trojan was a friend of mine, how can he take my girl from me?

"You have a girlfriend, Damien!" Trojan spoke, this time evil than ever.

"And you don't because you are not worthy off." I remarked, gritting my teeth.

He narrowed his eyes. "I want her!"

"I want her!" I cudgeled.

Malice made a mourned face. "Oh my goodness—I want only one lover, my Hunters. What shall I do now?"

I was filled with rage and hollowness. I don't know why, but I felt killing and ripping Trojan out. By Trojan's expression, I could make out that he felt the same tingling feeling.

"Let the bride decide, eh?" She spoke proudly. "We'll have a duel. Whoever will be the winner would be the strongest, and he would be my lover."

Our face got protracted. Trojan was grinning evilly, and I think I was giving the same expression. I took my sword out and he took his spear.

"Let the best win the duel." She said.

We ran towards each other…in rage and fury!

I never thought that I was weak, but seeing Trojan made me one. He was running like a wild tiger. His small curve muscles obtrusive, his face rampaged, his brows puckered with intensity, his vein filled palms clutching the hilt of the spear.

He immediately stopped, which made me surprise. I halted too. But his trick was too quick. He kicked me, collapsing me down on the firm floor.

I stood up, and rolled over as he tried to stab his spear towards my stomach. His spear jolted on the floor and got stuck. I stood up, and kicked him hard on the diaphragm making him fall down. I kicked him several times, when finally he surrendered.

His face was covered with blood, his body wounded.

Malice laughed, as she came towards me, caressed my cheeks and kissed me hard on the lips. It was unexpected, but it felt the best thing in the world. She parted her moist lips, and ordered me in a sweet manner, "Kill him, my darling. We will be happily ever after as it is shown in Faerie tales."

I ghastly looked at Trojan. His scared eyes watching my sweaty pulpy face, he was shivering. I saw something in his eyes, something which was one of the most peculiar things which a person has. I saw *innocence*, as if he was trying to tell me something with his eyes.

"Darling, my darling," Malice took my cheek, her blue eyes watching me, her soft palms touching my skin and giving me an electrifying feeling. "Kill him—he's no use to us. We will be happily ever after, happily..." I saw her lips moving rhythmically. "Ever After."

Happily Ever After, Happily Ever After...The way she said it, it was so alluring. Her coaxing voice reaching my ears audibly and giving enliven enticement.

She rounded her arms around my neck, and whispered at my ears, "Look at him...look at the person who wanted to kill you. Look how's he suffering when he tried to snatch me away from you. Look how he is struggling and trying to stand up. You are strong..." her hand went inside my shirt, touching my skin with her warm hands. "You are brave, my darling. Happily ever after, don't you want that?" She was now too close to my ears, that her tongue was barely touching me. "Don't you want what you desire the most? That is me, my darling!"

I came forward, making Malice leave her grasp of my body. I approached the struggling Trojan, who was looking at me with sadness, and innocence.

I took my sword, aimed at his stomach, and brought it up in the air. My eyes staring at his face...

"*Mate,*" His voice broke off from his mouth.

It was sudden. All the hibernated memories of Trojan came in my mind. And I did what was the best.

I turned and stabbed Malice in the chest.

She moaned...and fell down.

The sword was strung inside Malice chest as she strained herself to get out of the blade, but it was difficult.

"You fool…" her face had turned blackish and ugly and monstrous. Huge fangs erupted from her mouth; her skin became reptile green, her hair all thin and papery, and her eyes white and pale. She wasn't a beauty, she was a beast.

Her body started to vibrate, and then it started to produce vapors out. Her body was dead and placid.

I gave a hand to Trojan, and made him stand up.

He smiled, and we hugged each other. "How did you know that she was trying to play with your mind and tempting you to go against me?"

"I didn't."

Chapter - 21

The Secret of Bermuda Triangle

We finally found Elena and Tootsie in a small jail, which was at the end of the cave. Elena told us that Malice had fainted Trojan and me with her sting bite, and beaten Elena and Tootsie in a battle, throwing them inside the dungeon.

My gang reached the corpse, which was near the entrance of the cave. The corpse was now red, some bubbles shaking on the skin. Her face was now all bony, and was opened wide, with the freckles of golden hair (now white) laid on the skeleton.

Tootsie took a syringe out of her pocket, and inserted it in the fleshy part of Malice. I asked her, while the green slimy venom was coming inside the syringe's tube.

"Why did we only attack her for the venom? Aren't there any other Faerie in Lowlands?"

"Yes there are. But Malice was a Bollix leader, one of the most ruthless Faeries ever been evolved. Unfortunately she was my sister. Malice has the strongest venom inside her sting, stronger than any Faerie in Lowlands." She paused. "She tempts her enemies to become her lover. She has a power of persuasion and hypnotism which allows her to do anything with anyone. And in this case, I think the same happened with you boys as her magic of hypnotism works mostly on boys."

"Yeah, but when she said lover…I realized that I already had a lover…and a friend too…strong one's, you know. I don't know why, when I was going to kill Trojan, I just felt something different inside me. I felt as if I was going to leave someone. And then, when she kissed me, I remembered that there is someone who already has touched my lips…and then I realized…something which I never realized: Humanity." I smiled, as I wrapped Elena's waist. "I don't know why, but Trojan…" I looked at Trojan, then at Tootsie and then at myself. "We all think that we are different from Hunters. But we aren't because humans had taught us something vastly different, something which no Faerie, no Lucifer, no demon, no vampires, or anyone could understand. That's humanity. Today, I salute to it because it made me stop, it made me resist my emotions, and it made me *think* that I can't kill or cheat the one I love."

Tootsie smiled, "You know Damien…you are the first who had resisted the temptation given by Malice. You are the first one who had killed her." She shook hands with me proudly.

We raided back to the haunted mansion. I had sent a message by my Wiz Watch that we have found the venom and we are coming back safely. Osiris had foretold that Azazel has acquired the Black Skull from the Triangle and is heading back to the cave where it has all started.

We approached the haunted mansion where I saw Osiris and Athena, racing up and down the house in weariness.

"The earth's doom has begun. The Black Skull is in the

wrong hands, kiddo!" Osiris exclaimed as he paced around the room.

I was thinking calmly. I took the globe or in another words Trajectory Transmitter, and switched it on. I looked at the holograms where I saw demons and vampires pulling up the cords, settling the cargo, and handling the wheel.

I saw Flagon and Azazel walking up the board where a fearsome, tall demon stood with a skin color of green. He said, "The portal is near, master."

Azazel nodded. "How much time,"

"Almost one hour!"

"Good," his eyes bloodshot and dark, giving a strange look of anticipation. "Lour on."

I switched off the transmitter and asked Osiris, "What kind of portal is Azazel talking about?"

"A gateway which assists you in reaching Underworld back and forth, all the Dark Creatures get into Earth through that gate. It is called the Shadow Gates!"

I nodded, and ordered everyone. "Osiris and Athena, you go to Egypt and inform the Guardians about all the stuff is going on and tell them to come here:" I veered to Tootsie. "Do you have Faerie warriors?"

"Oi yes!" Tootsie grinned.

"Good, bring them to the Triangle." I stepped forth. "And inform them...the end is nigh!"

Osiris and Athena flew across Egypt. Athena was really fast, so she just whooped across the sky fields. Tootsie went towards the gates of Lowlands to inform other Faerie warriors about the war.

Trojan, I and Elena mesmerized how to work upon it. "We should be the first to strike them!" Elena thumped her foot. "We should crash their boat before they reach the portal."

"We need a secret plan to avert the ship till the real support of Guardians and Faeries approach. We need something which can haul the ship."

Trojan was flipping pages in some ancient books which were kept by Osiris in his study room cabinet. His eyes showed startling premonition, as he said, "Do you know the secret behind the Bermuda Triangle?"

I scratched my head, even Elena was puzzled by the question. "Large gravitational pull...perhaps."

Trojan squeaked. "No—the secret is Atlantis."

Elena and I gave confusing glances to each other. Atlantis was a place where Neptune or so called Poseidon sits and directs the sea. How come mythology has mixed in this world?

"No wait!" Trojan scratched his head as he read carefully. "It's not Atlantis...it's basically a place like Atlantis known as Palade which consists of Mermen and M-Mermaids. The place is the main source which generates..." he narrowed his eyes. "Generates the entire ocean of thy world—the Palade is under the direction of Titus, Mermen." His face alleviated."We can take help from him, mate. He'll possibly understand our situation and make them slow."

"How much deep is it?"

The idea of going underwater was really not good—for me. I mean, I had a bad encounter in the ocean in beginning of my new life. I also had a bad encounter with the evil Mermaids. And honestly speaking, I don't want to have another encounter.

But well, this is the end of world or the beginning of the end. I have to be brave about this.

"It's at the underground level, totally at the bottom of sea, there is an entire water kingdom formed." Trojan explained as he fidgeted by reading the book.

"Okay, so they would help us because they are good."

Elena repeated. "But how come we will enter their kingdom which is underwater to persuade them for the assistance?"

Elena had a point. We can't go several kilometers down with our human breath. We will eventually die due to choking and loss of air.

"It isn't as if Osiris has a pair of gills kept inside his study room." Trojan chuckled, after agreeing with Elena.

I got it!

"He has!" I spoke up, with a smirk smile on myself. "Osiris has Mermaid blood. He said that by drinking the blood in a soluble solution, we will acquire gills like a fish, but soon the gills will disappear, so respectively we have to do fast of whatever we will do."

"Who will go underwater and convince those human fishes that they have to save Earth from being chaotic?" Elena asked.

"I'll volunteer and plus I'm the captain." I gave a proud smile which was withdrawn from my face when Elena punched me.

I gave a low moan. I was being childish, I knew that.

Trojan backed off, "I will not do swimy whimy, mates." He was scared, terribly scared. "It's really…scary."

"What kind of pirate are you?" I said, disappointedly.

Elena remarked, "The thing is, someone has to watch the deck of Azazel's ship. It is because we have to know if he has carried out any attack or is he planning something out. Someone has to go by disguising themselves and become a part of crew."

"I can be!" Trojan whipped his hands up. "But I do not have Dark Creature characteristics in me." He said lowly.

I suggested, "Maybe he can watch with Gryphon at the top of sky with his binoculars and tell us important details through Wiz Watch while Elena and me will persuade the human fishes down at the kingdom as fast as we could."

Trojan agreeably nodded.

Elena and I went inside the study room leaving Trojan behind, where we started searching the cabinet which had most of the potions. Osiris hadn't taken all the potions in his potion holder waistcoat, so most probably; he would be having down in some compartment.

Elena was the first to find the compartment which had the holder consisting of hundreds of potions. We saw every potion, which was alike from each other. I asked sympathetically, "Are you sure that you want to do this, Elena?" My hands went round her waist.

She was scared, I could make out by her expressions. It was very deductively easy for me to read expressions according to the situation. But what I really liked about Elena is that she was scared but was brave at the same time. Her stern expressions, her pursed lips, her low brow tension, showed worry but heroism as well.

She took my arms and hugged me tightly, embracing the wretched hearts of ours and joining it into one. I hugged her back, rounding my arms around her back. I kissed her head.

I was defiantly worried about her. After all, she wasn't used to all this. Even an army girl can't handle magical situations.

"I am afraid, Damien." She pulled herself back, and looked deeply inside my eyes. "But...but..." she fretted her brows, and jutted her lips with her teeth as she continued. "This is *my* war too, Damien. I know the world doesn't know what the heck is happening around but I know—and if I know I have to prevent the actions which will happen which is better than being silent and imagining as nothing has ever happened."

I took a deep breath. I squeezed her shivery hands, and

embraced her again. She asked me, "By the way—do we have to drink a Mermaid's blood...literally?"

I was in the ocean with Elena. Elena, who I never imagined, was wearing a lace strapped top, which revealed her skin too much. She said it was because the swimming would be easier in light clothes.

So by listening to her advice, I did not wear any shirt on myself, and was bare chest, even I just wore my Bermuda shorts which were cut off till my knee.

Our bodies were splashed by the engaging water, as we floated. We could not sense the ground as it was dark, and I felt scared as I imagined that some sort of creature would erupt and will eat me alive (after all, we were in the ocean where Bermuda Triangle exists, one of the world's mysteries) .

Trojan was flying with Gryphon in the huge sky which was above. He gave a thumps up to us in assurance as we gave it to him in return. I felt a little jealous that he was only in air, and I in water.

Elena prompted, as she spoke difficulty, "let us drink the blood!"

I nodded.

My hand went down the Bermuda short pockets, and I pulled out a test tube which contained a different sort of color pigment.

Elena drank half of it (and gave obnoxious, frown expressions), I drank the other half.

The blood or the potion seemed tasteless, disgusting, and sour. When it reached my throat, and down at the food pipe, I felt as if someone was throwing fire. My stomach gave a gallop, and for a while, my body remained hot as ever.

"Nothing happened?" Elena asked, dourly.

"Nope."

Suddenly Elena started to shake. I got a hold of her bare arms. Elena was literally shaking as if some crumbling of crusts was forming inside her. Her arms started to change the shape. Well, her arms became softer, thinner, and more translucent. Small fins started to come.

Then it started with me.

I did not change like her. Actually, I started having some painful juddering on my throat. I touched it, and found a small, soft portion from which exchange of airs occurred.

"You have a gill?" Elena pointed.

I have a gill! I am a fish!

My legs started to vibrate. They automatically (I struggled) jointed themselves, creating a soft lower body like a Mermaid with a large caudal fin at the end.

Immediately, the fright and the fear of water were gone. I felt confident as if sea was my partner, and sea was my only life, and without it, I'm nothing!

Elena also started to get her Mermaid skin at the bottom with a fin. The difference between me and her was that, she looked hot, and I looked creepy.

We swam under the water, and to my surprise, I was easily swimming, under the sea stones and the boulders. I could visibly see the entire empty ocean with some fishes rushing here and there. But the most remarkable thing was the gills. I could breathe. I could feel that I could breathe. I felt oxygen pouncing inside my body and carbon dioxide poaching outside.

Elena spoke, "Can you hear me?"

"Yes, very suitably," I was surprised. It was so cool that I could hear underwater voice.

"Good, swim fast!" Elena said, as she rhythmically swam towards the bottom.

Damien Black
The Battle of Lost Ages

I followed her. Elena, to my surprise, was good at swimming too. Her movements of fins and her fish skin were so rapid that I could hardly follow her.

I had to break apart the water bubbles, and the water air, when I finally halted behind Elena. She fiddled her tail, as she pointed her finger towards the low lights which were occurring.

"Look, there's something shinning!"

"Palade," I mumbled.

I switched on the Wiz Watch and converted it into water mode. I spoke up into the watch, "Trojan, can you hear me?"

"Yup, mate!" Another croaking voice came from the watch.

"Listen, what do you see on the ship?" I asked, as Elena rushed over the small rocks, and overlooked the bobbing lights which appeared distinctly.

"Nothing much," He replied. "No suspicion movements plus no incoming. I could see that the shore to the portal is far off, so you have quality of time. Make the most of it."

I gave an okay-okay, and the switched off. I swam behind Elena, as she was ahead of me. She pointed her fingers, and said: "That's the kingdom, Damien…it's so big!"

I came to her point, and said, "Let's go!"

We came to the water gates which were guarded by two Mermen with tridents in their hands. They guided us into Palade without questioning to meet Titus the Director.

We saw many pavilions attached under the big dome. The dome was shaped in a form of a big pelvic fin as if someone had mistakenly architecture it. There were few shops and markets where dirty Mermen sold few water things. I even saw some Mermen who looked scholars to me, as they were intrigued in their own fantasy and talking about the disturbance which is creating the misbalance of the kingdom.

We came inside a big building which was supported by pillars from all side. The pillars were having entangled vines which rounded together, and touched the bottom.

I entered the building, which was little light but lots of human fishes. They all were chatting. Some were swimming up the stairs and onto the silk carpet. Some were intently watching the paintings on the wall. Some were looking up and seeing the ceiling's crafting.

Everything seemed quite interesting to me. I could not say how shocked I am right now. I feel as if I belong here, with these Mermen and Mermaids. It all looked so beautiful, partly because everything was under water and partly they were half fishes.

The guards took us up the stairs, and made us enter a big room where many Mermen with tridents were standing. There was a main Merman. Maybe it was Titus, as I could see his leadership and the authorities he showed.

He had a long white beard, and white fluffy hair, with cherished pink face. His fin and his Merman body was the largest of all. His caudal fin was at least bigger than my body itself. His eyes were icy blue, with lips as red as an apple.

"Captain, we have messengers." The guard said.

Titus stared at us for a while as if studying us. Then he waved the guards who went off, leaving the room. The other Mermen commander's were busy not to look at the teenage Mermen and Mermaid.

"I can smell your scent." He said to me and then turned to Elena. "Yours too…you are different."

What's with the smell, man? Every creature that lives on Earth or lives in Underworld can identify a Hunter by its smell. This is really irritating. If sometime I want to disguise myself, the creatures would find out immediately.

"We come with a favor which you cannot refuse." I said, acting like Vito Corleone in *Godfather*.

"And what is that?"

"Azazel...you must know?" I asked.

"Yes I know," he said lowly.

"Very well—he's trying to raise Lucifer. He has got the Black Skull, and he's now reaching the Portal."

A shot of intrigued pain was there in Titus eyes. His face became utterly red when he said, "The Black Skull was protected by the nymphs. I have very little idea about this. What is the favor, then?"

"The favor is that we need your help. We want to slow the ship of Azazel for a while and the other good army is coming for the rescue."

"So this is the reason for the putter misbalance and the disturbance which is occurring right now." He looked up at the ceiling of his room.

I saw the ceiling with Elena, and found cracks on it which were small but long and uniformed stretching from the ceiling to the walls and down at the ground.

He spoke, "They are creating disturbances on Palade. It is really a nuisance."

It seemed as if Titus wasn't taking this all seriously. He was lost in his own worry. He cared more about Palade than about the Earth.

"Will you help us?" Elena asked, as she wiggled her tail.

Titus gave a stern expression, not to us, but to himself. His hands shook in tension, as he spoke, "I cannot. I cannot risk Palade's life. Azazel would destroy me and Palade if I attack him."

"First of all, we are not telling you to attack him." I said. "We told you to stop him. You can hold the ship from underwater and make it slow as our army comes. Second of all, how can you be so scared of Azazel?"

"We had a war with Azazel and Lucifer many years ago. Palade was entirely destroyed. We supported the Hunters and we got destruction. Palade was far more beautiful than this. I cannot risk..." his eyes dropped. "I cannot risk Palade's life."

At his place, Titus was right. I felt brutally offended by his heart wrenching words, but when I saw his mourned face, and put myself in his position, I could see where it led. I would not help the Hunters if it would put my home in danger. I would have done the same.

"Titus!" Elena's voice shrieked. Everyone's attention was grabbed on to her when she spoke up. "If you don't risk Palade's life you will still lose it. Lucifer will rise if you'll not stop Azazel now. He will of course destroy Palade soon after as you would be few in number and no support will come."

I continued from there. "This is the time you can prove yourself Titus, the Palade's King. This is the time you can save Palade or lose it forever. We are losing time!"

One soldier under Titus said, "Captain, they are right. We cannot lose the most beautiful thing in the world just because we lost it one time before. We must fight every time."

"And not just for Palade..." another soldier came upon. "But for Earth also, because Palade is a part of Earth."

Everyone stood in support and revolt. Titus looked at every soldier, scholar, and commander. All were bravely humming a sweet melodious tone which somehow meant:

"O hails Palade, the mighty kingdom. We shall oath today that we will protect it and prevent it from any gruesome attack by our enemy."

I came in front and said, "We must protect in which we live. We must fight for it even if we are scared to lose something." I looked at Titus.

He understood what I meant.

He lifted his arms, with an expressionless face and said loudly, "Let's stop the bewitched Dark Creatures."

Chapter - 22

The Battle of The Seas

Titus and his army of Mermen with Mermaids did something very clever. They did not proudly and stupidly attack the ship of Azazel, but instead they grabbed the edges of the ship under the water. With all their might force, they tried to stop it. Unfortunately the ship didn't halt at once, but it slowed down.

Our powers of a Mermaid were long gone now, and we were behind the ship, resurfaced at the above. Trojan came up with Gryphon, and got us upon it.

Elena and I were shivering. We were too long in the cold, icy water. Elena grabbed my body, and hugged it profoundly by explaining that it would increase the warmth inside both of us. She was at some point right because, a tingling warm feeling started to build in the temperature of my body.

We saw the small figurines which were all around the ship, under the water, and grabbing it with their hands as tightly as they could.

Azazel and his soldiers were pretty confused of what was going on. One of the commanders gave a sighting view at Azazel and told something which was not audible. Azazel angrily stamped the foot in frustration.

Flagon, Azazel's dragon moaned, which was overheard by us.

Gryphon spoke up, "I can translate to you on what is going at that deck."

"Please, tell!" Elena whimpered as she crossed her arms around my neck, getting closer to my back.

"The commander of the ship whose name is Gorgon had proposed or assumed that the gravitational pull which is very frequent in the Bermuda Triangle is occurring, which is causing their ship, *Argon* has slowed down. Azazel is angry about it, and even his dragon is angry."

I switched on my Wiz Watch, and contacted Osiris on it. I spoke up, "Osiris?"

"Yup, kiddo," a hazy voice spoke up; maybe the voice was blurry due to the technical problem.

"Where are you?"

"We are near…we are going to cross Santo Domingo now." He said.

"Cool, the progress is going good. We are winning according to me.

"Good, good. Keep it stands by, we are coming."

Gryphon yelled, "Guys, I think Azazel saw us."

We looked down at the deck and saw Flagon and Azazel staring up at the sky. Azazel was narrowing his eyes as if trying to see if it a big bird or a griffin with three people sitting on it.

Azazel immediately raged. He called up Gorgon, and pointed his fingers towards me. Gorgon with an unexpected shock ran towards to his soldiers. The soldiers looked up at the sky after Gorgon told something to them, keeping an eye on us.

The soldiers got their bows. They perched upon the board, near the swinging leather ropes. They pointed their arrows towards us...and yea, they arched us.

Gryphon gaped through the air, and wound up in the misty clouds so the archer's couldn't see us. Unfortunately, we couldn't also see them.

I could hear the yells and screeches from the ship. It was horrific and at the same time exciting.

Then the screeches increased, and all of us exchanged glances. We came down, winding the clouds away, and saw Osiris on a Pegasus.

Athena was flying individually and was blowing fires from her mouth at the top deck and the poles. The archer's ran all the way, escaping the fire.

Azazel said something to Flagon. The dragon squeezed and pressed himself hard in the air, to ultimately duel with Athena alone.

We even saw the Guardians with their Pegasus. They all were carrying magnificent lusting spears in their hands, clutching hard to it. The spears weren't normal ones; they looked quite heavy and were doubling bladed with a height of five inches at most.

The spears were producing electrical lights, which gave tremendous shake to the ship.

Ahmad with his Phoenix, Delilah was also there. He came upon us, and said, "Hola, guys!"

We waved hands to him.

We all were winning. It seemed so easy to defeat Azazel.

But I wished I would have not been wrong as the next attack was unexpected. Azazel sends his riders on black small winged dragons that flew in the air, with their swords.

Azazel then ordered his archers to shoot the shadows

which were stopping the ship (in another words, the Mermen and the Mermaids)

The archers, instead of pointing at the top in sky, started in the water, where the shadows lay. I could see the arrows being stung in some of the Palade's life form, who floated and were vaporized in water.

Azazel was clever, really clever.

I ordered Gryphon to take me down. Trojan also detested himself to come with me and fight on the *Argon*.

I persuaded Elena to stay on Gryphon as it could be difficult for her to defend her life on the deck. When she protested, I had just said that she served Earth at the utmost purpose.

Elena embraced me, and even Trojan (a friendly one, as I shrugged my shoulders that time in deficiency). Gryphon made us land at the lower deck where the archers were aiming the water.

Gorgon and Azazel weren't visible which the good thing was.

The time we landed, Trojan and I started using our armory as fast as possible. The archers (who were mostly weak demons but good at shooting bows) gave an astounding sanctum as we stabbed our sword and spears inside their chests, stomachs, eyes and heads.

Some of the archers in east pointed the arrows, aiming and shot it immediately towards me. We dodged the incoming arrows fortunately.

Then I took my gun and shot bullets at their heads in a sadistic way.

Trojan went towards the upper deck where the swordsmen were getting ready for the battle. Trojan stabbed his spears without fear of death. For the first time, I saw Trojan's intensity in a fight...in a true Hunter's way.

From the lower deck, where gallons were positioned, Minotaur's and Cyclopes pounded. Minotaur's with their buffalo head, and a human body, and Cyclopes with a human body but one eye in the center.

Cyclopes shouted. "Die...dies!"

They looked up at the Guardians and saw the enormous lightning bolts they were producing and hitting on board.

The demons took flaming arrows and pointed at the Pegasus. They all shot the flaming arrows which spread in the entire sky, making half of the white shinning Pegasus wounded.

Some Guardians fell down into the water, brutally wounded; some just wound up in the sky and then crashed in the depths.

Osiris was trying his best with Ahmad to fight. Delilah was throwing fire balls at the decks which were prevented by the Minotaur who just whisked his hands in front of the fire and it got deflected as if he was hitting a normal, softball.

Then Osiris with his staff gave off light which blinded most of the demons and the vampires. Even the Cyclopes were blinded. They were thrown at the back, and half of them fell down the ship, drowning to death.

The Minotaur didn't look at the enemies with his eyes. He actually hears the sound with his big flapped ears.

He rushed towards me. I rolled over my body, and immediately skit off, shooting bullets at his back. Minotaur didn't get hurt by the bullets. He stumbled upon a demon that was carrying an axe in his hand. He snatched away the axe and came towards me.

Meanwhile, Athena raced in the air with her angelic wings, as she gapped through the clouds and the skies. Flagon the dragon was following her, and blowing out smokes of fire out of his mouth.

Athena gave a quick U-turn which astonished Flagon

at the spot. Athena rounded back, and then with all her force, produced fire from her mouth, creating a circle of flame around Flagon and entangling him into it.

The Minotaur destroyed the shaft with the axe as I dodged all his attacks. I do not know how I could possibly dodge a Minotaur's attack that was once (according to Greeks) defeated by Theseus.

He smashed the axe blindly at some of the galloping demons, making them collapse on the ground. In another words, the blind Minotaur was useful to me.

Trojan from the upper deck, jumped with his spear uplifted in his hands. He stings the spear inside the human body flesh, creating intense pain for the Minotaur.

I immediately pointed my gun towards the Minotaur's heart, as Trojan was stabilizing him. I shot several bullets at his chest, making him fall down with Trojan beneath him.

Trojan finally got up and sighed in relief as he removed the saline sweat from his forehead.

The demons with swords and axes and sabers came towards us, smiling ferociously and angrily.

We gave nervous glabrous to each other...

On the other side, Faeries of different sorts, shinning and having butterfly wings were being guided by Tootsie. The fallen Guardians who were barely defeated with Osiris needed urgent assistance.

Tootsie ordered the pixies to attack the borders of the ship where gallons were being prepared by the lower deck demons who were trying to demolish the flying Pegasus and the Guardians which flew near the ship.

Tootsie then ordered the normal sort of Faeries who could easily fly and demolish the dragon flyers. Then she herself helped Osiris on the side.

Damien Black
The Battle of Lost Ages

Her army of Faeries gave us a lot of advantage.

Athena turned her position towards the ship where she saw Osiris battling with the vampires who were sitting on the dragons. The other Guardians were trying to kill the demons and the Werewolves from west side, coming from lower deck.

Athena came towards the deck, her wings flapping enormously, as she fled just few meters above from the broken shaft shouting at Trojan and me, "Jump!"

We didn't understand what she suddenly meant, but then we did. Flagon shot fire balls towards Athena, but he was a stupid dragon as he didn't realize that Athena was flying just above the ship.

We jumped inside the chilly, icy waters. Athena gobbled up in the air, eluding the attack by coming up in the air.

The fire balls created gargantuan explosion which annihilated most of the ship into pieces. The ship was almost wrecked as the Mermen and Mermaids from Palade attacked it by jumping on the wrecked ship, and attacking the demons and vampires.

Elena took us with Gryphon in the air, as we were all saved, and fortunately saved the Earth too. I gave a glance around, and found Azazel nowhere.

Ahmad with Delilah came up to me as he yelled in excitement, "We did it, guys!"

"Can I get Delilah for a moment?"

Everyone was tremendously shocked!

"Why?"

"I feel something. Please it's urgent."

Ahmad with a trusty look nodded his head. We exchanged our rides. I didn't take Elena or Trojan or Osiris with me this time.

Inside my mind, I could feel, the same man with wings, Dogma yelling and shouting saying, "Damien you are the winner! Go…and kill Azazel! He's just reached the portal."

I aviated in the air with Delilah. With the help of leathery threaded saddles which gave me good support, I drifted with no problem yet I didn't know the way but Dogma was directing me, telling me where the portal really is.

I took Delilah towards Puerto Rico's island, where some kids and parents were playing in the pool happily; not knowing anything of what trouble is going in this world. I then turned towards a mountainous forest which should be El Yunque according to the geography I had learnt in school.

The mountains and the forest were only visible from the above. As I went below, I touched the canopies, and break through the branches, putting Delilah's feet on the clustered leaves.

In front of me, there was a willowy waterfall which swung the water insanely and dropping itself inside a pond.

I saw Azazel's ride, and even saw Azazel who didn't notice my incoming here. He was literally walking inside the small pond, and entering the waterfall, with his winged dragon, Flagon. I thought that Flagon was killed by Athena, but that really misunderstood me.

I left Delilah near the waterfall, telling her to wait for me. Then I went inside the pond, and entered the waterfall.

Chapter - 23

The End

I was in a room…or so I thought I was. This was the portal, right?

Entering a water fall from a mountainous forest area, and coming up in a new land entirely, made me feel quite weird, I don't know why. I looked around the room, and saw that I was in this place before—the same place, I don't know why, but I feel that this place is familiar somehow.

There was light darkness in the room, and a throne stood in the middle with some stairs ascending to it. There was silence creeping all over the place, and which gave chills and shivers.

Behind the throne, stood a big tomb made of marbles and granite. The edges were designated in a shape of a skull, and on the front, the tomb was carved of different, ancient designs. Some carvings were round and made of sun; some were carved as a moon.

I came to get a good view of the tomb, but then I saw Azazel sitting and kneeling next to it, with a shimmering crystal skull in his hand. The skull was black, entirely black, and it glinted with intense fury. The bones, and the upper head were small, but the lower jaw of the skull was big.

It lay motionless in Azazel's hand, as Azazel murmured few omens. His eyes were closed, and his mouth hummed, with his one leg kneeled on the floor and other up in the air. His hands displayed the skull to the tomb.

He was practicing a ritual!

Then I realized!

This is the same place which Dogma shows me of Underworld. This is the same place where Azazel was being directed by Lucifer himself.

This is the control room of Underworld.

I went towards Azazel, keeping a tip toe, and being silent. The subtle nigh gave me chills, as I took my dagger, and then with all might force—I stabbed Azazel's back whilst he practiced the ritual.

Azazel with a sudden shock tremendously aroused. The dagger was stabbed inside his spinal cord, making his entire body shake.

I pulled the dagger back, as he fell down—on the ground.

He looked at me, with littering red eyes as he said, "Damien Black, what a nice surprise?" his voice was choking.

I was just meters away from him, and he could easily kill me, but he didn't. He laid himself on the ground, shaking his body, and speaking to me in a cold, killing voice: "So you have come to your home, eh?"

"I don't call this home." I whispered—as my breath was tired.

"Your father did," Azazel spoke. "He always did before he was in temptation with your Hunter mother." His face grimaced.

"You expect me to be like my father?" I sarcastically asked. "If he lived today, he would never want me to join."

"Yes, he had foretold me that he didn't want your

destiny to be like his. But unfortunately he died and his death increased the pain in every Dark Creature, especially in me." I narrowed my eyes, when I heard the next sentence. "Because I was *his* brother,"

I fell back on the ground, skit away from his conscious laid body. I was in utter shock. The pounding of my heart was beginning to jostle incredibly.

"Yes, Damien…" he stood up, with his hand around his back. "I'm *your* uncle, your real one."

I took deep breaths. This was getting way too complicated for me.

Flagon stood behind me, with his wings flapping and his nostrils flaring. He didn't attack me, he just saw my cowardice within me.

"You never asked that why your guardian Osiris didn't tell about your powers before so you can practice it and master in it? Did you ask him this?"

Honestly I didn't ask Osiris. I never did. Why? Because it never came up in my mind or was I too scared to know?

"Osiris is a good wizard. He was beholding your responsibility till your death. Osiris wanted to hide these powers because he knew that your subconscious cannot hold the demon which you have inside yourself. By not telling about your powers, you would never get your evil side heavy on you. But now as you have known your powers, you will soon be *with* us."

I wanted to protest and fight with him. But then, a sudden hulk hit my chest and I felt an urge to be with him, be in this mighty place where Lucifer the Creator Underworld is going to rise.

I came in my senses. I was becoming different. I have to stop being of whom I am really.

"Your father didn't have a name—it never did." He said. "He was called Demetrius here. But when he fell in love, and married your mother, going against our codes, he changed his name to Black which was your mother's actual name."

"My destiny is to kill you," I stood up, with my dagger in the hand. Flagon charged but Azazel waved at him. "And prevent Lucifer from rising!"

"You can be much greater than anyone — even Lucifer." His eyes were filled with greed and obsession. "Be with me, and I will teach you to be the greatest of all, to be the real king of Underworld." He paused. "I never wanted to kill you, Damien — I wanted to capture you and convince you in believing me that I can be the one for you — I can be the real mentor, real guardian."

"My destiny belongs to finish Underworld." I said. "You cannot convince me. Everyone believes in me — Elena, Dogma, Osiris, Trojan, Athena, Ahmad, Tootsie, Titus."

"You will die soon if you take that path. You will be forgotten. Right here, if you stay with me, you will be a legend to all the Dark Creatures, you will be a barbarian of Hunters." He added. "You think Dogma the Helper trusts you?"

"He does, he has been guiding me all the time."

Azazel laughed. His eyes started to burst water. He clenched his stomach, after a long wide mouth laugh and said. "Dogma isn't what you imagine, Damien. What do you think? Dogma which you see in your dreams is actually the real Dogma?"

"Yes, of course!" I exclaimed.

"No you fool!" Azazel shouted. "It's Lucifer!"

I narrowed my eyes. "What?"

"Lucifer is Dogma, Dogma is Lucifer. The man who comes in your dreams isn't the real Dogma, it's a disguise made up by Lucifer. He has a power of mind control. He can go to any mind and control its sub conscious. He knew about your powers, about how strong you are. He even wanted to massacre you as he felt that you can be the only one who can stop him and kill him but I gave him a choice: What if Damien Black himself becomes a part of Underworld? Lucifer was happy. He spoke to me that he will play with your mind. He will manipulate you." He explained as my body felt numb. "You remember the zombie attack? You know why I sent it? It was because Lucifer told me so. Lucifer himself told that he has to make you trust in him by showing you the truth. Lucifer also conducted the town Vampires to kill Trojan as he wanted all Hunters to die. But he didn't tell about you which led to complications.

"He said that your powers were taking control on your mind. He couldn't control you anymore. He wanted you to get away from the Hunter path and he wanted you to make him think in that way. And you did—you thought about it. You fell in love, your puppy love, and you realized that human life is better. I felt bad. I wanted you to be with me but Lucifer had its own plans. He later on said that you are totally under the guidance of good and you can't be tamed as a Dark Creature because you found something: True Love. I protested and I promised Lucifer that you can change. That is why I sent Nosferatu, Damien—not to kill you but slaughter Elena. Take her as bait, and when you come to rescue, kill Elena and take away you." He paused; his eyes were filled with tears. "But you won. You didn't change. I gave you last chance now; Damien or unfortunately—Flagon will kill you."

A soaring voice came from the back—and I pretty much knew that it was Flagon's breath which surrounded me.

"One thing I never understood—why do Hunters kill Dark Creatures?"

He quizzed his brows.

"Well—because—we want to rule Earth—this universe—and Hunters prevent that from being as they think that humans are worthy more than us."

I stumped my foot...and jumped!

It wasn't really a jump...it was actually I could fly. But then I found my body decreasing in altitude. I came upon Flagon who struggled.

As I tried to control Flagon, my mind was just looking the days back when Dogma directed me. He was a liar. He was Lucifer and I couldn't believe it. I felt pain, but not because I was being used but because I had trust on him.

One thing I had learnt now—Trust is not an option.

I took my dagger as Azazel leapt towards me. I stabbed the wailing Flagon as it immediately collapsed on the floor, unconscious. Azazel's leapt was of no use as he fell somewhere else, I rolled over somewhere else.

I changed my dagger into a sword, and said, "Let's fight like a gentleman, shall we?" I gestured my sword.

Azazel looked at his dragon, and his eyes filled with tear. He was having humanity in him, he was having emotions—he was just scared to face them.

He took his spear which was laid next to the tomb. He kept the Black Skull, on top of the tomb, as the winner will take it.

He pointed his spear towards me—and we began.

We rushed towards each other, then suddenly he crouched, skilling his spear on my knees, making wounds on my skin. My legs felt numb for a moment, and a sting of pain was really biting.

I didn't care as aimlessly I dueled with him. I jutted, poked, stabbed, and swu'ng my sword as fast as I could, but Azazel was dodging every attack of mine as if he knew every move of mine.

"I feel bad for you, Damien." He said, as he móved round me, some meters away. "You chose the path which is already lost."

"A lost path can be found—if you try." I said, and suddenly attacked but he deflected my sword with his bladed spear, and then swift his spear nears my stomach, which I fortunately do2dged.

I rolled over to his back, when he suddenly turned himself—and he attacked my face. I kneeled down at that time, and I kicked him—which made no affect.

I started remembering the time when I had a friendly duel with Osiris. That time, I still remember, I had a different kind of power—which made the time slow, and which made me attack faster than Osiris.

Was that my demonic power?

If it is a coincidence, then I must not concentrate, but if it isn't, then I have to think about that power and make it useful as I'm losing here now.

I jumped back, and closed my eyes as Azazel ran towards me. I thought about the slow time, and for a while, nothing happened. Osiris had said to me, that my powers will work if my entire focus lies on it.

I opened my eyes after the focus. And I saw Azazel about to stab me in the stomach—but he stopped—no waits—he slowed. He became so slow, and his spear was clunking towards me in a very slow motion. I thought that this power is actually slowing the time, but then I realized that it didn't slow the time, it just made my reflexes so fast, that I could see everything slow.

I dunked my sword inside his chest, which passed through his back—and then the slow motion stopped, and he fell with perspiration.

He couldn't stand up as his body was weak and timid. He was having difficulty. I spoke, "I AM NOT PROUD OF HAVING AN UNCLE LIKE YOU!" I pointed my Beretta at him—when I fainted!!

Chapter - 24

The Fall of Lucifer

I opened my eyes — and found myself in the same place which I call Paradise every time and where I meet Dogma or Lucifer every time.

But this time the place wasn't like Paradise at all. The willows, the trees, were broken. The meadow, where above it, Lucifer and I flew was now entirely destroyed — bursting into flames. The sky was thunderous, exploding lightning bolts every second. The grasses were being moved, and were twitching due to the heavy grasping wind.

The place was a disaster — it was turning into hell.

I walked past the landscape where once the sun met. The horizon was nowhere seen, and the heavy, dark clothes clotted the entire sky. I walked towards the small cave, which was under the long logged terrains — when I heard…

"Damien Black!"

I turned back.

It was astounding that I saw Dogma, with his wings, and his cupid face walking towards me. His face was peaceful as always, his body elegant and his eyes cherished with sympathy.

"You know the truth now—ah?" He asked. "That I am your archenemy."

"Yes, but you are nonetheless never going to rise."

I saw a frown on his face but then it vanished. He said, "I am here to warn you, Damien Black. Your uncle, your sick uncle, wanted me to make you an apprentice of mine. I was reluctant as I had different choices. I wanted you away from my path, and so I wanted you to fall for Elena and live like a human life. But then, I gave another thought, and I realized, you can be useful somehow and I listened to your uncle. I told him to kill Elena and capture you as I can convince you and make you a fellow student of mine but you are filled with love, gratitude, emotions…" he said as if the word 'emotion' was the most disgusting thing in the world. "You are a human in other words. Weak, pitiful, humble and gentle…the characteristics are really bad. If you want to fight me at the end—you must forget all these. And I'll be waiting for your signature to be on the Scroll of Death when you would choose the path of dark."

"At least I have something which you don't and will never have," I said bravely. "But when you rise, till then, adios."

I hurt his feelings and I could see his furious eyes, filled with anger and rage which he tried to contemplate and control.

"I warn you, Damien Black." He angrily pouted. "I warn you. I will come back and kill you, but for now—I can only say one thing—the Battle of the Lost Ages—has started."

I did not know what he meant…

I woke up!

I saw myself in my haunted mansion's room—fully protected and blanketed. I felt warm and good. For the first time, I had a feeling of peace.

Elena was looking at me, brushing her hands through my hair, smiling at me, and giving mischievous looks yet it looked graceful on her beautified, angelic face.

"How are you?" She said.

I touched my body—it felt weak and tired. "Yeah, I'm good." I lied to her.

She kissed me on my forehead, and came on the bed with me. She hugged me tightly, breaking my bones, but still I hugged her back, as I could feel a little love after a long battle which we all won.

"We saved you. We couldn't let you go alone by yourself. We followed you and saw that you had defeated Azazel. We took away the Skull as well as you, and left the place." She explained. "The *Argon* was completely destroyed and all the creatures were dead. Osiris has destroyed the Black Skull which was the only fear that could raise Lucifer. Now everything is in peace and harmony, Damien. Osiris told that by devouring the Black Skull, we have destroyed the portal of the Underworld, and that we have no fear of any Dark Creature perching upon Earth again."

My heart lit up...

Finally we won, we won!

It felt the best thing. Everyone safe and sound, my family was safe and even Earth was safe. There would be no damages in the future, and there would be no supernatural phenomena.

"Damien," she patted my shoulders. "The Fall of Lucifer has taken place. We have won. We have won!" She kept her head on my chest.

I met Osiris later on, who happily hugged me. He was with Athena, sitting at the porch and reading a magazine. For the first time, I had seen him reading a magazine which he didn't even understand.

He said that the world is safe and there is no threat. He also said that I could end up having a new human life which I always wanted.

I was joyous about it.

"You never asked why I didn't tell about your Dream Travel powers before." Osiris said with a spontaneous smile on himself.

"Why?" I was excited to know.

"Because Damien, you have a blood of a demon. By increasing or letting you know the characteristics of a demon, you will yourself be possessed like Rolf was. I wanted you to be like a pure Hunter or somehow want you to *know* that you are a pure Hunter. Now it's up to you. If you can resist the temptation of evil, it would be the best but if not, we will hunt you soon."

"Osiris, I know that but, you do not have to worry about me being evil. Because my greatest enemy became my sign of supremacy," I smiled.

Later on, I met Trojan who said that he is partly joining the crew of reanimated Blackbeard who will sail the seven oceans.

I learnt further that Gryphon had left; Tootsie became the queen of Lowlands. The Elder Guardian was dead and so Ahmad took his place. He was known as the youngest Elder Guardian now.

I joined the school back with Elena, and we happily lived after. We mostly missed Trojan on the way as he was gone away for a while. Our romantic session began once again, and we left what we faced before.

There were questions which weren't answered to me till now like what was the Battle of Lost Ages? What more powers I have about myself? Why I was called the Prince of Darkness, is it because of my demon blood? And are there more Hunters like Trojan and me living on Earth?

Chapter - 25

Unfinished

I was in my sleep when I found myself inside Underworld again. Not again! I mourned.

I gave a brief look at the Underworld and found that it was empty, isolated. Then I realized that I actually am present inside the control room, where Azazel stood!

I couldn't believe it—I thought Azazel was dead—how can that be possible? I had killed him by myself.

He was standing next to the tomb. But now his face was all disfigured, with a huge hump on his back, which made him a hunchback. His eyes were crooked, and his body was big and creepy.

He was looking at the tomb for some hope when it gave a shinning glinting light to it.

I looked at Azazel smiling with devilish happiness. The tomb started to shake, and then the cover of it—moved.

Oh my gods!

It literally moved. From the tomb, a hand popped out.

It was a fleshy hand with long nails. The entire body came out and I saw for the first time—Lucifer's real face.

He wasn't like Azazel or any other demon. He wasn't a demon actually or a vampire or a werewolf or any Dark Creature. He was greater than any of them.

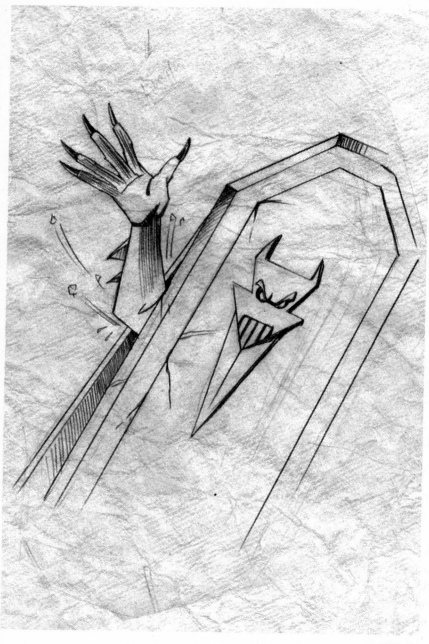

His eyes were pure white. His horns were almost five inches big, and his body larger, taller (almost 12 feet). He had wing large red wings on him, and his body color was dark and brisk, glowing with redness. He was bare chest, with abs and muscles coming out like a rock.

He smiled, "How did I rise, Azazel?" He said in a husky, deep, devilish voice. "What kind of secret omen you used?"

Azazel was bowing down. He replied, "I had practiced a half ritual on you which raised a part of you. But the powers which you had before are now gone, and are still buried as the other half is still inside."

"At least I have risen." Lucifer smiled.

Lucifer looked at the positive side of his fall. He said, "So shall we begin our invasion?"

"Uh...uh..." Azazel hesitated. "Well, the thing is, master—that I feel really good that you have risen but—but the Black Skull is destroyed and the portal of ours is also gone with it. We do not have any means of entering Earth now."

Lucifer was plain blank for a while. His eyes showed tension but he didn't react. He just moved back, looking at the wonderful shinning tomb as he said, "So this is it, Azazel. We have to summon him for the last time."

Azazel crowingly said, "Are you sure, master? Is this the right timing?"

"It is—we have to call Soul—my monistic brother now."

Soul...Soul...the same guy...the same who is pure evil and stronger than any matter in this entire universe—he is Lucifer's brother!

"And this time I'm planning to take over the universe as Soul had once said *oorwin die heelal* which means conquer the universe—and now we shall begin to do it." He moved towards me—as if he knew that I was standing and listening to their conversation right now. "If Damien Black or anyone listening and hearing this, I must foretell you—*this is not the end.*"

Damien Black
The Battle of Lost Ages